All The Cowboy Wants

Rhonda McKnight

ISBN 9798526878524

All The Cowboy Wants

Chapter 1

Addison Ingram believed in love.

For other people.

Other people managed to find it and keep it, so maybe they deserved it more than she did.

Her eyes swept the cabin of the Bennett jet, taking a quick inventory of the couples on board—the people who had found love. Her sister, Harper, and Logan Bennett were sitting in a corner, inseparably hugged up like people who had been married less than twenty-four hours. Her bridal bouquet rested on the table next to them. It was still fresh from yesterday's ceremony. Her sister, Rachel, was sitting on her husband, Zeke Bennett's lap. They'd only been married a little over a year. They hadn't come down from the newlywed high yet. And finally, there was Cole Bennett and his beloved. Every so often, he squeezed or stroked his fiancée, Lenise's knee like he couldn't stop touching her.

Yeah, she believed in love. It was all around her—in close proximity, but not in her life. That's why she was annoyed by the question Avery Bennett had just put to her. Addison gave her friend a wry look. "Why would you ask me when I'm getting married? I can't focus on a relationship until I achieve some level of success in my career."

She'd practiced that response—a lot. To emphasize her point, she pulled up her work email on the iPad she had on her lap. It was true that her job took priority, but the success she was reaching for eluded her. Her boss was intent on holding her back, and Addison took it personally. She read the email that had just come through from the woman.

"What the devil?" Her boss had to be kidding. Addison typed a reply to the message:

I will not be a part of this story in any manner – that includes research, interviews, or editing. I am a serious journalist, and I will only cover serious stories. You can take this one and shove it where the sun doesn't shine.

Avery craned her neck to read Addison's words. She hiked an eyebrow that made Addison question her loyalty. "Are you going to send it…with that cliché in there?"

"The conversation we're having is a cliché. Why are you asking me about marriage? I'm not even dating right now."

"Touchy much?" Avery tsked. "Your sisters are ticking themselves off the singles' list one by one. I thought it might be a virus running up through the family." Avery sipped wine and took a selfie. "Forget I asked."

"I just did."

"So, back to the email." Avery glanced at the iPad again. "Are you sending it?"

Addison squinted at the screen and erased the message. "No. I'll wait to have a face-to-face meeting with her—where I'll basically say the same thing."

Avery took another picture. This time it was of the wine bottle. She updated her business social media pages like a rabid teenager. "What exactly is she asking you to do that's unsuitable for a serious journalist?

"It's a silly story." Addison sighed. "The magazine is covering the top ten bachelors of Atlanta. They want me to write a part of the feature."

Avery snickered. "What, are you on punishment or something?"

She didn't mean any harm, but her laughter pricked Addison's nerves. "It's not funny."

"You're right. It's ridiculous. Do women still read that kind of stuff?" Her friend looked disgusted.

"They do, and they enjoy it, and look forward to the issue every year. With sales going down due to digital, we have to sell every hard copy we can. We only release a print magazine quarterly as it is."

"So what are you going to do if she insists?"

"Make my editor keep her promise. She told me when I came on that she needed me to write a fashion column. I understood that. It was my background, but I was clear I wanted to get out of fashion as soon as possible. It's been two years. She moved me out of fashion, but I'm still doing the Metro Happenings column. Events and grand openings, and God help me if I have to go through another season of indie theatre and movie screenings, I'm going to go crazy."

Avery dropped her head on Addison's shoulder. "You should come work for me."

Addison peered down at her. "Doing what *this* month?"

Avery smirked. "I'm into this winery thing I've got going. Don't act like I'm flaky and irresponsible."

"You're neither flaky, nor irresponsible, but the wine interest might evaporate the same way the spa franchise and the coffee thingy did." She shrugged Avery's head off her shoulder and stank faced her. "What made you think you could grow coffee in Montana?"

Avery raked a hand through her thick, black hair and slipped Addison a side-eye. "Why are you bringing my past up like this?"

"Because your past wasn't that long ago." Addison chuckled. "Girl, I have to have a stable job. You can play these games. You're rich."

She snorted. "I'm not rich yet. I am still just a Bennett trust fund baby. I have yet to reach my twenty-eighth birthday, so my inheritance is collecting interest."

"Poor you," Addison teased.

"Well, it's true, but I'm also young, so I have time to find my passion."

"When you find it, if it happens to be a magazine or a newspaper or even television, let me know and then I'll come work for you. In the meantime, I have to figure out how to tell my boss I'm not doing this."

"Just say 'no,' girl. Say it like you'd say no to crack." Avery giggled. She was half drunk. "I have to pee." She stood and put her glass on the table.

Addison was seconds from telling the passing air steward to bring her a glass too. Instead, she looked up at the group again. Everyone was exhausted. They'd all been drinking at the wedding reception and now they were drinking on the jet. She couldn't blame them. The wine—courtesy of Avery's vineyard—was superbly rich and intense. But Addison was staying sober. She wasn't riding home in the convoy of limousines they'd reserved. She'd left her car at the airport.

Stone Bennett caught her eye. He balanced his large, cowboy-booted, right foot on his left knee. He wore jeans, a simple white t-shirt, a slick, leather blazer, and an expensive looking cowboy hat. Stone always wore cowboy boots and a hat because he was a real deal cowboy. It made him stand out from among the Bennett men.

As if he'd sensed she was staring, his eyes popped up and met hers. A devilish smile crinkled the corners of his eyes. Addison returned her attention to her iPad. Heat filled her cheeks. The kind of heat that got a sister in trouble. She raised her arms and pulled her long, curly hair into a high ponytail and forced herself to focus on the next email in her queue. She tried to concentrate on work, but she could still feel his eyes.

Stone was always doing the most in the staring department. It wasn't a creepy, weird, stalker stare. It was more of an all-consuming stare, like the negro was trying to figure out how to snatch the wind straight up out of her chest so he could possess a sister's mind, body, soul, and common sense. She hated that he unnerved her so much, because he seemed to sense it and took her refusal to engage with him as a challenge.

Addison knew the type. She'd dated a few. Men who always got what they wanted because first of all, they were fine—definitely true in Stone's case. Second of all, because they had that swagger—Stone got triple points for that. Finally, third of all, they were successful—again, true in Stone's case. She'd lived in Forest Hills long enough to know that rich kids lost their fortunes all the time to bad investments, gambling, and drugs. The word on Stone was that he was quickly moving toward billionaire status. The man knew where to put his money.

Why had God made some black men so handsome and sexy and desirable? It made no sense, especially since most of them weren't ready to commit to anyone. Jesus had some explaining to do. This mess down here was not cool. Not cool at all.

Addison removed her phone from her bag and placed a call to one of her coworkers. She wanted to complain about the assignment some more, but more importantly, with Avery gone, she needed a distraction. The last thing she wanted Stone to do was catch her looking at him again, and he would if she didn't find something else to hold her attention. God help her. She was drawn to him.

"Always the wrong man," she whispered to herself. "I am always looking for trouble."

Chapter 2

Stone Bennett rubbed his forehead. Addison was finally off the phone. He'd been trying to get her attention, but as usual, she was ignoring him. She was ignoring everyone in favor of her iPad.

He raised his glass and took another sip. He'd be about half drunk by the time he finished it. Drunk was unattractive and unattractive was the last thing he wanted to be right now. The flight steward approached, carrying a tray with bottles of water on it. He waved him over.

"Take this." Stone put his glass on the tray and took one of the waters. "Bring one of those sandwiches, please."

The attendant was back in moments with Stone's request. Hoping to sop up the alcohol, he ate quickly. Then he rose and went to the restroom to brush his teeth. He couldn't get Addison off his mind. Like all the other Ingram sisters, she was beautiful, but Addison's extra bit of fire had always sucked him in. Although he was glad, he couldn't believe she was still single. The men in Forest Hills and greater Atlanta were dumb and blind. Who wouldn't want her on his arm and in his bed?

He remembered how he'd caught her in the corridor at the reception, pulling her dress down from her waist. Those legs. He suppressed a groan. He felt heat rise throughout his body. Addison had been doing that to him for years. It was time for him to get what he wanted before one of his cousins did. He stood and walked to the empty seat beside her.

"Avery's here," Addison said, letting her eyes dance between his and the chair.

"Avery doesn't own this jet." Stone dropped into the seat and perched his elbow on their shared armrest. "Besides, she's in the cockpit, flirting with the captain. I know my cousin. She'll be a minute."

Addison pulled her torso back, away from him. "What was wrong with where you were sitting?"

Stone frowned. "Jesus, Addison, you could at least pretend to like me."

"Why, because we're related by marriage?"

Stone chuckled. "Don't try that. We are not related by anything but our humanity."

"My sisters *are* married to your first cousins."

"That don't make us kin." Stone tapped her wrist with his index finger. "There's no blood between us, and you most definitely do not feel like family."

Addison let out a chuckle. "What do you want, Stone, besides the obvious?"

"There is no obvious. I just wanted to sit next to you, like I did when we took baptism class together."

"Well, there's no workbook here for you to cheat off of."

"I wasn't cheating. I was checking my answers against a more credible source."

"I was eight and you were what...sixteen?"

He massaged the back of his neck. "You were not eight."

"Yes, I was." Addison scrunched up her face. "If you don't admit that you were copying, I'm going to put my earbuds in."

"Why are you blackmailing me? That was over twenty years ago."

She reached in her bag for her ear buds, and he placed his hand on top of hers. She'd been teasing him, laughing, but when he touched her, their eyes locked, and he felt what they'd always had—chemistry. Stone didn't know about her, but he wasn't getting enough air in his lungs.

"Okay. I won't force you to confess. It's not like we don't both know the truth." She pulled her hand from under his. "Tell me, what have you been up to these days?"

"Lately? Getting horses ready for the WPRA."

"Must I Google to find out what that is?"

Inevitably, his eyes strayed from hers to her lips before he forced them up again. "The Women's Professional Rodeo Association. There's a competition in Franklin. It's in a few weeks."

Addison's smirk was knowing. "Cowgirls. It figures you'd have your hands all over that."

"Anything men can do, women can do ten times better," he said. "Cowgirls need support. They need more than the men."

"What do you do to prepare?"

Stone enjoyed watching the curious writer in her come out. "I have a full-time vet on staff, so we provide medical certifications for the horses. It's required annually and more than annually for some events. I board the horses who are in transit and provide a place for cowboys to work with their animals."

Addison continued to look at him like she was waiting for more, so he gave her more.

"Everyone doesn't provide friendly service to cow persons of color. I get involved in a lot of the invitationals. I have a foundation that provides financial support."

She looked impressed. "Do you still compete?"

"Nah, it's been years for me. I was done when I hurt my back."

She nodded like she remembered that.

"Don't get me wrong though, it's still a strong back—useful in many ways, just not worth ruining by competing. I have enough trophies and belt buckles to let it go."

Addison tossed her head back and whispered the word, "Right." Then she dropped her eyes to her tablet.

Avery bounced out of the cockpit. She took the seat he'd vacated just like he'd asked her to when he'd texted her. But the flight wasn't much longer. It was *go* time. If he was asking her out, he needed to do it now. Stone crossed his arms and watched her work for a minute before saying, "Can I have your attention for a moment?"

Addison's head came up. Green flecked, cinnamon eyes melted into his and he lost his words to his heartbeat.

"I'm not interested, Stone."

That was cold. He dropped his arms. "You don't even know what I want."

"I've always known what you want, and the answer is no."

He frowned. "You have to eat. Why won't you have dinner with me?"

"Because it would be a bad idea."

He cleared his throat, adjusted his shoulders, and tugged at the lapel of his jacket. "Why? You're attractive. I'm attractive. In fact, I'm extremely attractive, and I'm good company."

Addison laughed. "You're also conceited."

"What's wrong with a little conceit? My parents were pretty. They made pretty children." He flashed a playful smile. "You're beautiful, Addy, but you have to admit, I'm special."

The hint of a smile remained on her face. "Stone, you're a lot. I only date with intention. It's not like I could get serious with you."

She'd said a mouthful, but he was far to intrigued to give up. "All kidding aside—and I was kidding— why couldn't you get serious with me?"

Addison gave him her full attention for this part of her response. "You're a Bennett. There are enough Bennetts married into my family. And even if you weren't a Bennett, you're insanely rich. I don't want the headaches that come with your kind of money."

"You're going to cross me off your list because I'm too rich. Where do they do that?"

"I do it. I'm flattered. I think…but I'm sure I'm not interested. I'm a simple woman who wants to live a simple life and aside from all of that, I'm not even dating right now."

"None of this makes sense, but not dating during the prime of your life…that really doesn't make sense."

"Why would now be the prime of my life? If I live to be ninety, I'd hate to believe I hit my prime at twenty-eight."

"I believe our prime can last a long time. Like twenty-eight to sixty."

"Then it seems I should be able to take a year or two break from dating."

Stone pondered that for a moment before responding. "I suppose you're right, but herein stands the dilemma. I'm interested in you right now."

Addison shrugged. "Like I said, I'm flattered, but the answer is no. It's always going to be no." She smiled politely like she hadn't just cut a brother down to the size of airplane peanuts and returned her attention to her work.

Stone went back to his seat. He distracted himself with a conversation with his cousins, but his eyes never wandered far from Addison. This time, he was more discrete. He stole his glances carefully. He chuckled to himself. If Addison thought he was deterred by her little "it's always going to be no," she had another *think* coming. He might be a man without a plan right now, but that was temporary. He always got what he wanted. She would find that out soon enough.

Chapter 3

"Addison, be a team player. I only need you to interview one of the guys. The others have been assigned to Josie."

"Why couldn't this last one be assigned to her too?"

Addison's boss, Beth Knowles, popped out of her chair, flipped her thirty-inch Remy hair weave over her shoulder, walked to the coffee maker and poured a cup. "Because he couldn't be."

Addison let her mind race through the reasons why: *Josie was overwhelmed?* Never. *Josie knew him?* Possibly. *Josie had dated him?* She thought about the female version of Clark Kent who sat a few cubicles over from her. No way Josie had dated a man who was one of the hottest bachelors in the city. "Can't you just tell me why?"

"I have my reasons." Beth handed her a file before reclaiming her seat. "And since I'm the boss, I get to hand out the assignments as I see fit."

Addison opened the skinny folder and flipped through the information. She hated these kinds of stories. They were embarrassing to add to her byline. "Where's his name?"

Beth sat. Avoiding her eyes, she said, "You'll learn it when you meet him."

Before she could stop herself, Addison rolled her neck. "Why?"

Beth took a sip of coffee. "Because that's the way he wants it."

"How am I supposed to prep, and why is he calling the shots?"

"He wants the interviewer to meet him cold so you can get a real first impression of him."

Frustration gripped her throat. She tried to clear it, but it was no use. Her words sprang from her mouth with more of a bite than she intended. "Beth, are you serious?"

"I am. He's never been interviewed. Getting him in this piece is a win for us. He's different in some ways you'll understand when you meet him." Beth picked up her cell and dialed a number. "Do a good job." Dismissing her, she spun her chair away from Addison.

Addison rolled her eyes and left the office. Great. She got stuck with the jerk in the pile. She dropped into her chair and picked up her phone. The telephone number in the file was a north Georgia area code. She dialed it, got a nondescript voicemail, and left a message.

Three days went by. Addison was tired of calling this guy. He wasn't calling back. Just as she was about to storm Beth's office to tell her about her interviewee, her phone rang.

"Good afternoon, may I speak with Addison Ingram?"

It was a woman on the phone.

"This is Addison."

"You've been attempting to reach my boss for an interview for your magazine. He's available to meet with you this evening at six pm at the Warm Mountain Ranch in Mountainville. That's Union County."

"Tonight?"

"Will that work for you? If not, I have a few other dates."

She needed to get this over with. "Tonight is fine, but I thought he lived in Atlanta. This is a feature about Atlanta bachelors."

"He spends most of his time up north."

Great, I get the rugged bachelor.

"He's made arrangements for you to stay overnight."

Addison frowned at the phone. "Overnight?"

"Ms. Ingram, it's over a two-hour drive from the city."

Of course it was, but it was a lot for him to presume she wanted to stay. She forced a smile into her voice. "How will I know him?"

"He'll know you. There is a restaurant in the lodge. You have a six p.m. reservation. Valet parking has been prepaid. I'll email you a confirmation." The call ended.

Giving into her mood, she slumped in her chair. "I have to drive all the way to Union County to meet with a hunk of meat." Addison Googled Warm Mountain Ranch. "And I'm meeting this dude at a literal dude ranch. He's already tired."

She waited for the email confirmation and forwarded it to her boss before walking out of the office. It was almost lunchtime. She decided to go home and get ready for the trip. Her shoulder length curls needed a wash and retwist. That would take a few hours. She wanted to get up the mountain road before dark.

She and her sisters owned a cabin in Blairsville, Georgia. Her parents purchased it a few months before their death. She hadn't been up there in over a year. It wasn't really a place any of them spent a good deal of time, but they couldn't let it go. It had sentimental value. It was only an hour from

Mountainville. She could have stayed there, but Mister "I'm in Control" already made arrangements for her. But that made her think, her guy wasn't just a handsome bachelor. He was one of the bachelors with money.

Once her hair was dry, Addison loaded her laptop and overnight bag into her car and got on the road. The ride was long, but easy and uneventful. She enjoyed the view and a good audio book along the way. It was pretty in this part of the state. She couldn't deny that.

She pulled through the main gate, up to the valet parking area, and handed her keys to the attendant. Once he confirmed her name was on the list, he opened the door for her, and she walked into the main lobby of the resort. The entrance to the place was cut in half. One part was an elegant waiting area with an overhead chandelier and wrought iron benches made from smooth, glossy pine. The floor was a polished tile. A rustic, cattle ranch sign made of aged, galvanized metal hung on the wall behind the benches claimed establishment in 1937.

The other half of the lobby housed a gift store that looked like it threw up touristy trinkets. There were ornaments and magnets and carvings of horses, cowboy, and native figurines. Not the cheap ones you got from Dollar Tree for…well a dollar…but fancy etched metal and glass keepsakes. There were also postcards and bottles of wine. Lots of wine.

In contrast to the slight chill outside, the atrium was warm and woodsy. Dead animals hung on the walls next to lit candelabras. Welcoming music piped through the speakers. The aroma from the restaurant caused her stomach to stir and beg to be filled. She looked at the time on her phone. She was twenty minutes early. She decided to let the *maître d* know she was here anyway.

"Ms. Ingram, please come this way," he said, escorting her toward the back of the restaurant. They passed all the diners and went to a private room. She expected to be seated there, but then he pushed open patio doors. A horse drawn carriage was waiting. The driver jumped down and extended a hand to help her up.

Addison frowned. "Are you sure this is for me?"

The *maître d* replied, "We're quite sure. Enjoy your dinner."

Addison hesitated. She felt like she was in danger of being human trafficked. She had no idea who this guy was. She'd called an untraceable phone number, talked to an unknown woman, and had been given instructions to meet an unknown man. But who would make her come all the way to Union County to be kidnapped? That was easy to do right in Atlanta.

She accepted the driver's hand and stepped up into the carriage. After a few seconds, the driver hiked the reins and the carriage lurched forward. The sun had gone down, but even in the dark, she could see the grounds were amazing. She'd never been to a dude ranch.

After a short ride, she arrived at a small, free-standing cabin with a large, covered patio that was twice the size of the building. It included a firepit, huge leather sofas and a dining table complete with a white-gloved server. The driver stopped the horse and helped her down.

She took the few steps up to the patio and watched as the carriage disappeared in the direction of the main lodge. She turned to the server.

"Good evening, Ms. Ingram. May I offer you a glass of wine or some other beverage?"

"Water will be fine," she replied, fighting more frustration. She'd had enough of this guy's anonymity.

"How boring is that?" A male voice came from behind her. One she recognized. She turned. Stone Bennett.

"Addison Ingram. Aren't I lucky?" Stone's smile was wide and amorous.

"Stone, what the –"

"Watch the language. You're on the clock."

"You? Why?" She paused for a moment, trying desperately to gather her thoughts around this ruse. "Since when are you willing to do an interview?"

"I lost a bet with the owner of your magazine. We went to college together. My ante was this feature."

"You went to college with Tom Schuller?"

Stone nodded. "He's a friend."

She planted a hand on her hip. "You were just in Forest Hills. Why did you make me come all the way up here?"

"Because I didn't want to be interviewed in Forest Hills. I wanted to be interviewed here. On my own turf, so to speak."

Addison dropped her hand from her hip. She might as well get this over with. "Are we eating out here? It's chilly."

"It's fifty-nine degrees, but it's not cold over here." Stone spun in the direction of the table. He pulled a chair out for her. "Come on in."

Addison looked around, specifically eyeing the firepit, and realized he was right. She wasn't cold, but being outside made her feel exposed and naked, especially since he'd caught her off guard. She slid into the seat. Rather than take the chair across the table, Stone sat next to her, which was close. He bumped the side of her knee getting situated.

"This is business. I'm not here to be entertained. I'd prefer to be inside."

A little smile played at the corner of Stone's mouth. He looked toward the server. "Miss Ingram will have a glass of wine. I'll have a vodka neat, and we're ready to dine."

Addison raised a hand to get the server's attention. "I said I wanted water."

"This resort has the most delicious muscadine wine in the world. The grapes are grown locally, and it's made right here on the property. You'll love it." He looked to the server again. "In case I'm wrong, bring that water too."

The server nodded and went into the cabin.

Addison put her bag on the chair on the other side of her. "How do you know I like muscadines?"

"Writers aren't the only ones who do research."

Zeke. He and Rachel brought her a bunch from some organic market Rachel visited in Hilton Head a few weeks ago. Addison pulled her phone and a small recorder from her bag. "Do you mind if I record you?"

Stone pushed his back into his chair. He removed his cowboy hat and placed it on the empty seat next to him. "I do."

Addison smirked and reached back into her bag for a notepad and pen. She swiped her phone and pulled up the email with the questions she'd prepared.

Amusement filled his tone when he said, "I hope you don't think I'm going to answer questions on an empty stomach."

Addison peered at him. "I was hoping you would. I'd like to get home."

Stone frowned. "You're staying overnight."

"But leaving early in the morning." She put her pen down. She could see he wasn't going to be moved by her urgency.

"Not too early," he said, cocking his head. "You'll need time to get to know me."

"I already know you."

He leaned close to her ear and whispered, "No, you don't."

The server returned with their drinks and placed them in front of them. Stone raised his glass. "Let's toast."

Addison picked up her glass. She didn't think they had anything to toast to, but she was getting paid for her time with Stone, so she indulged him. "To what?"

"To my liking what you write about me."

Addison pushed her glass in the direction of his. "To you cooperating." They clinked them together and both took a drink.

She took another sip. The wine captured her taste buds and slid down her throat like the silkiest of drinks she'd ever had. She raised the glass. "You were right. Very smooth."

Stone smiled. "The vodka is equally good."

"Don't get drunk. If you give me the material for a tell-all book, I promise you I'm going to write it."

He chuckled. "No one would want to read a tell-all about me. I'm not that interesting."

Addison took another sip of her wine. "Why did you really agree to do this interview? 'Atlanta Bachelors' is not really the way I'd expect you to break the ice with the media."

"I don't know. Maybe I'm looking for a new circle of women to choose from."

She looked around like she was expecting to see one of Stone's girlfriends, but they were the only two people in this area of the resort. "Have you bedded everyone up here in Union?"

"Not at all. This area is ninety-eight percent white. I like my women Black mixed with more Black."

His velvety voice dropped to husky when he said that. The glint in his eyes was mischievous, but authentic at the same time. He was a ridiculous flirt. Adrenaline coursed through her veins. Addison raised her glass and took another sip of wine to help with that. "Is this your place?"

"No. I own a ranch about seven miles down the road."

"Why didn't you just have me meet you at home?"

"Because writers are smart. If you had the address, you would have looked it up and known who you were coming to see. Even if you were lazy and didn't bother, which we both know you're not, you would have known it was me when you arrived. Diamond Bennett Ranch is on the gate." He took another sip of his drink. "I wanted to be a surprise."

The server came back through the doors with salads and bread. After he disappeared, Addison asked, "Was all this cloak and dagger really necessary?"

"Yes. Mr. Bennett didn't know your preference." He refilled their glasses and also put tall glasses of iced tea on the table.

She wrinkled her nose. "The salmon will go to waste. Why didn't you just ask?"

"It won't go to waste. I'll send you home with a doggy bag. Better than a chick bag, right?"

She couldn't help rewarding him with an amused smile. "The steak is fine. I can't say I've ever had a cowboy ribeye. What's different about it?"

It was Stone who smiled now. "It's big."

Addison realized she'd walked right into that one. "Oh, the symbolism."

He chuckled. "I'm a big man. I like big things."

She couldn't resist teasing him. "Compensating?"

"I cannot tell you how much I'd like for you to find out." Cockiness curved his lips. "And I'm not scared to disappoint you."

Addison's face warmed red. She hoped the low light from the candles hid it. She picked up her silverware and began to eat. "Seriously, you are going to have to answer my questions, so go ahead and tell me why you're a cowboy."

Stone cut a huge hunk of steak and put it in his mouth. After chewing he said, "I love horses."

Addison shoved a piece of asparagus into her mouth. Stone swiped béarnaise sauce off her chin before she could raise her napkin.

He tasted it. "Just the way I like it."

Addison wiped her mouth. "This is why I don't eat while I interview people."

"Sure you do. Aren't you always interviewing people?"

"No. I ask questions, but it's not an interview." She took a sip of the iced tea. "Owning horses is great for someone who likes them, but an entire ranch seems extra."

"Is there a question on the table?"

"Why do you own a ranch?"

"Because I like horses. It's that simple. I like training them and being around them."

"Well, tell me—"

"Uhn, uhn," he said, wagging his fork like it was a traffic sign. "It's my turn to ask a question."

Addison pulled her head back. "I'm not being interviewed."

"Sure, you are. I want to know more about you, so you ask a question, I ask one."

"I can't promise I'll answer."

"I can promise you I won't if you don't."

She sighed and threw her hands up. "Go ahead."

"When did you know you wanted to be a writer?"

"I've always been a writer. Most writers will say that. I lost my job with the stylist I was working for when he closed up his shop. I saw a posting for a fashion writer for the magazine and decided to shoot my shot. They hired me on the strength of my fashion background and my writing sample."

"The story you did about Zelda Wynn was good."

"What part did you think was good? The fact that she designed the original Playboy bunny costume?"

"The fact that she was the first Black woman to open a shop on Broadway. I also loved that she did so much for Black designers during her rise. The collaborative aspect of her legacy was interesting, especially during that time-frame." Stone cut into his steak again.

Addison tried to hide how impressed she was with his answer. If he was trying to show an interest in her work, he'd done a good job. "Well, she was in New York. It wasn't the Jim Crow south."

"Still, it couldn't have been easy. Nothing has been easy for our people," Stone added. He took another bite of his steak. He wagged his fork. "The Playboy bunny thing was interesting too."

"I loved researching her. I interviewed a few members of her family."

"You said she was your favorite person to research. Why?"

She tapped the table. "It's time for me to ask you a question."

"I'll answer two in a row." He said it like he was negotiating a contract. She let him have that. She loved talking about Zelda Wynn.

"Very little is known about the early, Black fashion designers. Most were just referred to as seamstresses. She was a true pioneer."

"I just had a God-given talent for making people beautiful." Stone raised his glass and took a sip. "Her words."

Addison was impressed. "How did you find that story? I wrote it years ago."

"I read it a long time ago. I've read quite a bit of your work."

For some reason, her heart began to pound. She almost didn't want the answer, but she had to ask. "Why?"

"Because I've always found you interesting, Addy."

"Stone, you're full of it. You don't expect me to believe you've been following my columns."

"Oh, but I have. I've followed them since you began. I remember when you took that break two years ago." Stone put his fork down and picked up his drink. "You went to Central America for a few months."

She swallowed. "Nicaragua."

He nodded. "To teach English to the Afro-Nicaraguans, right?"

Addison resisted showing shock. No one knew that except her sisters and the people who read her column to the fine print. "Who told you that?"

"It was in your column," he said. "What made you do that?"

She felt tension fill her belly. Not because of why she'd gone, even if the trip was birthed in misery, but about why Stone cared to know. "I needed a change."

"From what?"

Addison picked up her wine glass and finished it. "Forest Hills." She knew her response only elicited more curiosity on his part, but she wasn't going to share more. "You owe me two answers."

Stone drummed his fingers on the table before picking up his fork again. "Ask away."

The dinner progressed with Addison learning several interesting things about Stone that she didn't know. He'd also done a good job of interviewing her and finding out all the details about why she was doing this interview, and what she hoped to write once her editor took her more seriously.

She couldn't finish the huge steak, so when they were done, Stone asked the server to bag it up and include dessert. The carriage reappeared. Stone stood and took her hand. "Come on, I want to show you something." He took the wine and two glasses and helped her into the carriage. The driver moved the carriage forward, away from the ranch and into a wooded area.

"We aren't going to get eaten by a mountain lion?" Although she was certain Stone would fight a lion with his big, bare hands, she asked anyway.

"Don't worry. Jake and I are both packing a piece." He opened the bottle of wine. "I'd never let anything happen to you."

Addison slipped back into her days as a little girl, when she'd gone hiking up at their cabin with her father. He'd assured her he wouldn't let anything happen to her. A man hadn't done that in a long time. Although she was feeling strangely odd from the rush of emotions, she held up the glasses for him. "What are we going to see out here?"

He poured the wine. Put the bottle in the ice chest and pulled the heated blanket over her legs. "Be patient."

They rode about fifteen minutes before coming to a clearing with a waterfall. The full moon shone on the rapidly cascading water, creating a rainbow of turquoise, blue, and gold on the frothy water. They exited the carriage and walked closer to the pond.

Stone squatted and picked up two smooth, black stones. He stood. "This is Horse Trough Falls, named by the Creek Nation natives who resided in the region."

"What does this feed into?"

"The Chattahoochee Watershed. Chatta means "rock," hoochee means "colored" or "painted," and the combined word means "rock of many colors" – the Indian name for the river. It was also Cherokee land at one time. The Creek Nation natives, now known as the Muskogee, believed if you threw a stone in the water at night on a full moon and made a wish, it would come true."

Stone looked at his stone. He rubbed it a little, raised his arm and pitched it into the water.

"You seem to have everything. What did you wish?" Addison asked.

Stone smiled, but it wasn't as wide as it normally was. "I don't have everything." His words were somber and longing. He handed her a rock. "Your turn."

Addison stared down at the rock for a moment. It felt heavy in her hands. She wanted to believe in the magic power it was supposed to possess, but she dismissed it. She raised her eyes to meet his hopeful ones. "I don't believe in wishes."

"Not even a little?"

She shook her head. "Not even a little."

"You could wish for the perfect story when you're done with me."

"My success is dependent on my hard work." She handed him the stone. "Maybe you should make another wish." She turned her back and walked toward the carriage. "Maybe you can wish for world peace."

Stone's smile shone in the moonlight. He raised the stone to his heart and then tossed it in the water.

Addison climbed back up into the carriage and pulled the blanket up around her legs. She waited for Stone to join her. But she was anxious to get as far away from him as she could. Her hotel room was calling her away from this handsome, sexy, virile man who had set up the evening to be more like a five-star date than the setting for a magazine interview. No wonder he had women clawing at each other. Sexy wasn't just how he looked; it was how he operated.

Her insides had melted when he started talking about the Native Americans. Nothing turned her on more than a man who respected culture. Black mixed with more black. That was still swirling around in her head. She wanted to be like Cinderella and tell this carriage driver to hurry and get her away from this ball.

They rode back to the lodge entrance and got down from the carriage. A big, fancy pickup truck was parked in the opening. Of course it was his. He was right. Everything about him was big...big feet, big hands, big spirit, big laugh, big spender...big, big, big. He pulled the door open on the passenger's side.

"Stone, it's late. I really am ready to go to my room."

He hitched his thumb in the direction of the lodge. "Oh, you think you're staying here? You don't have a room here. This place is full."

"What do you mean?" Her heart knew before she asked the next question. "Where am I going?"

"To my house."

Still, she shook her head. "What?"

Chapter 4

"What kind of game are you playing?"

"No games here. The lodge is full. All the hotels are full. The music festival begins tomorrow. It's an annual event. It draws thousands to the area." Stone rattled off the explanation like he was a local expert.

Her lips twisted with disapproval. "Are you kidding?"

"I have a good-sized house. I didn't think you'd mind staying in it."

"You made a big assumption." She stepped closer to the truck, but stopped before getting in. "Where's my car? I'd prefer to drive it."

"Are you going to be pissed when I tell you it's at my house? It's with your doggy bag."

She pursed her lips and hopped into his truck. He closed the door behind her and pulled away from the lodge.

Addison Ingram was stubborn. He knew that, but he was finding it more attractive than her face and body. He hadn't expected that. She seemed about as interested in him as she was in a bag of horse manure. He hadn't expected that either. He adjusted his rearview mirror before sliding an eye in her direction. She had her elbow resting on the window. Her head was resting against her fist. She looked like a child on punishment. It made him wonder if he had overplayed his hand with this idea to bring her to Mountainville, but then he dismissed his doubt. His confidence kicked in. She just had to get to know him better. She'd never allowed herself to do that.

The light wind blowing through the slightly cracked window blew against her hair and he caught a whiff of coconut. He'd seen her with pressed hair before, but he liked that she wore it curly. It gave her face character and made her stand out from the many women he'd dated who liked their hair down to their behinds. She was drop-dead gorgeous. She always wore shiny lip gloss on those full lips of hers. They called to him, begging him to kiss them.

He'd long returned his attention to the road, so when he glanced in her direction again and found her looking at him, he felt that familiar stir in his gut. The one that was never wrong about women. The one that said, "She wants you too." She cut her eyes away from him, but it was too late to deny, she liked what she saw too.

Addison glanced in Stone's direction like she was wondering if they were parting ways. He wasn't nearly ready to let her go. "I'll show Miss Ingram to her suite when she's ready. We still have some work to do." He slid her bag off her shoulder and handed it to Swenson. "Please put this in Miss Ingram's room. We'll be in the theater."

Swenson nodded. "I'll bring in refreshments." He walked away.

"Refreshments? I can't eat another thing."

Stone reached for her hand and pulled her in the direction of the corridor that led to his home theater.

She fell into step next to him. "How am I working if you gave him my notebook?"

Stone leveled his gaze in her direction. "Something tells me you have a great memory."

As they walked down the hallway, Addison stopped to look at some of the art on the walls. He had canvases of famous cowboys and cowgirls framed. Some were originals and others were reproduced for his collection. Most were of Georgia rodeo competitors. Mixed in were some impressionist pieces from Black artists.

"You have quite the collection." She crossed her arms over her chest. "How big is this house?"

"Ten thousand square feet."

She lifted a brow. "Zeke lives like a pauper compared to you."

"Zeke used his money to buy a soccer team. Property in Forest Hills is expensive. And my side of the family has more money."

She seemed amused by the last statement. "Zeke and his siblings are your poor relations. That must mean you and your brother are almost billionaires."

He chuckled. "Don't forget about my sister."

"Trinity? I could never. Where is she these days?"

"Last she checked in…Eritrea."

"Doing what?"

"Buying frankincense, I think." He opened the door to the theater room and turned on the light, and then hit the switch for the fireplace.

Addison put her hands in her back pockets. She inspected the room with interest. It boasted a massive OLED television and six rows of reclining leather theater seats. The flooring was cranberry red and cream tiles. A polished, black, vintage popcorn machine was installed next to the bar. There was more art, which she looked at with interest. When she was done, she walked to a recliner and plopped down. "What are we watching?"

Stone fell into a seat next to her. "Whatever you like. Rom-com, action adventure, suspense, the local news."

"Where's the remote?"

"It's voice activated."

Addison's eyes widened again before sliding away from his. He was starting to feel like a showoff. "Love, turn on the TV. Open the guide."

The screen flickered and came on. So did the guide.

"Love, scroll films."

A long, alphabetical list of movie titles rolled down the screen.

Addison angled her body away from him. "Why are you using the name Love?" Her eyes burrowed into his, demanding an explanation.

"I like it better than Alexa and the other ones."

"Interesting." She crossed her arms over her chest again like his answer wasn't sufficient. He didn't know if that was a habit, or if she was sending body language that indicated she was "closed" to him. Based on her expression, he'd guess the latter.

"This will go on all night," he said. "Can you pick a genre?"

She reached for her ponytail holder and removed it, letting her curly hair spill around her face. He liked that.

"You choose," she said. "It'll tell me something about you."

Stone rubbed his hand down his face. "Love, select *Harlem Nights*."

Addison frowned. "I haven't seen that since I was a teenager."

Stone pushed the button to the recline his seat. "I love Eddie Murphy, Richard Pryor, and Red Foxx."

"Other than Eddie Murphy, you're too young to even know most of their work."

"Too young? Are you kidding? I've watched everything Richard Pryor's ever done. He was a master."

Stone lowered the seat separator between them. Before Addison could protest, the door opened, and Swenson entered. He carried a tray with popcorn, salsa and chips, fruit and cheese, a beer and a glass of wine and put it down on a tray table that rose from the floor at the push of a button on Stone's seat.

With Swenson's exit, the lights dimmed. The film began.

"This evening is feeling more and more like a date than an interview." Addison reached for her wine glass.

"Maybe you can report what a great first date I am."

She pursed her lips. "You know that might not be a bad angle." She set her eyes straight ahead on the screen.

"I told you I wanted to go out with you," Stone said.

Addison slightly careened her head in his direction and then turned her attention back to the screen. "Aren't you lucky to have gotten assigned to me."

"Might be luck. Might be fate."

They both stuck their hands in the popcorn at the same time, touching briefly and setting off an electric charge that was undeniable. Addison pulled her hands back to her lap and didn't move them again.

Stone watched her for a long time. She'd been easy to be with once she relaxed her suspicions about him. Although it was his house, they both had better energy now that they were away from their respective families. Other than church, Bennett and Ingram gatherings or events in Forest Hills were the only places he'd ever been around her. They relaxed and fell into easy conversation. Both laughed heartily at the movie, but close to the end, Addison began to yawn. She'd had a long day with the travel, and she'd had her share of wine.

When the film was done, Stone switched to the local news. Addison murmured, "Just let me have a five-minute nap before I have to walk to my room." She folded her hands under her cheek and closed her eyes. It was only a few minutes before she shifted and moved closer to him. A few minutes more and she was curled up next to him. Her hair smelled like fresh coconuts and her perfume, a fruity scent, mixed with it and kept his senses lit all night.

As Stone watched her sleep, an unfamiliar ripple of emotion coursed through him. It was something beyond sexual attraction. It was strong, overwhelming, and had been growing in intensity by the moment. He pulled his eyes away from her. He groaned inwardly.

She's getting to me.

This was not how it was supposed to be. This was not what he was expecting. It was time to put her to bed.

Stone stood, scooped her up in his arms, and carried her out of the room. She woke for a moment, and he whispered, "I'm taking you to your room." Addison raised her eyes to his, nodded, and laid her head back against his chest. He'd expected a fight to get down, but instead, she raised a hand to his shoulder and pressed into him.

She stirred a little when he placed her on the bed. She'd already taken off her boots in the theater room, so he pulled a blanket over her. After a few minutes of staring and wishing he could climb in with her, he lowered the lights and opened the door to leave.

"I'm glad you're not a twisted stalker who watches women sleep." She called out from the bed. She laughed a little, rolled over and said, "Good night."

He chuckled. "Night, Addy." He pulled the door closed and went to his own bedroom.

Chapter 5

Addison woke. She found herself staring at an unfamiliar trey ceiling. The wood was intricately carved, ornate, and rich. She pushed herself up and looked around. After shaking off the fog, she remembered she was in Stone's house, or if she was being accurate—his mansion—where ceilings cost more than a year of her pay.

She scanned the bedroom. The space had a sitting room, a masonry fireplace, and a large screened porch. She could see the lake on the other side of the walk-out terrace. If this was a guest suite, what must Stone's own room look like? Maybe he'd give her a peek. She was curious about his hat and boot collection. There had to be enough leather in there to outfit most of the cowboys in the southeast.

There was a clock on the nightstand. She noted the time was three a.m. How had she gotten in here?

She hadn't remembered walking to her room. She scooted off the bed, found her handbag on the desk. She removed her cell and went into the restroom. She stripped out of her clothes and came back out to find her overnight bag. After slipping a night shirt over her head, she bunned her hair like she did on nights she didn't want to retwist it, and covered it with her favorite bonnet. Then she climbed back into the enormous, comfortable bed.

More out of habit than curiosity, she checked her email. Harper had sent one along with five text messages asking her where she was and why hadn't she answered the previous messages. The first message included a link to the wedding photos.

"Finally," she muttered. The photographer had taken forever to finish the retouches.

Addison clicked on the link and began to browse through the pictures. Harper and Logan's choice to marry at Logan's hotel in Puerto Rico had been the right decision. The pictures were gorgeous.

She found herself lingering on a few of Stone and then lingering even longer on the ones of herself with Stone. There was one of all the Bennett men sitting in a row of chairs with cigars in their mouths. It was unique and sexy. She knew Stone smoked a cigar and a pipe. He hadn't last night, but she'd seen him do it at a few events. Ordinarily she didn't like smoke, but she found a cigar or a pipe a little sexy in the hand of the right man, and Stone was definitely a man who made both look good. She looked through a few more pictures and found one of him and her coming down the soul train line. He was silly, but fun. A warning went off in her head. Her heart rate was abnormally high right now. She looked around the room some more.

What am I doing in his house? In one of his beds?

"Don't do it, girl. Don't let him get in your head."

She needed to get out of here as early as she could tomorrow, but he hadn't given her nearly what she needed for the interview. Not even close. She had a whole list of questions she had to ask him for the feature. She put down the phone and turned off the light. Sleep came hard, but the realization she was attracted to Stone Bennett came harder.

***

Addison never had trouble sleeping, but this waking up on a designer mattress thing was heavenly. She threw her legs over the side of the bed, stood, and stretched. She picked up her phone and walked over to one the windows. Both had window seats, something she'd always wanted, so she happily sat on one and opened the shutters. This was some good wood. She didn't know why she was up in here trippin' on all this fancy material. Rachel's house was beautifully furnished. She'd also spent many hours checking out the houses Harper decorated, including the ones she visited on the set of the *Atlanta Home Designers*. But there was something about owning a space this luxurious, even if it was temporary, that made her feel like royalty.

She opened her phone and smiled at the picture of her nephew, Christopher. Rachel sent one every morning. He was eight months old now. Just the age when they were yummy, and he was looking more and more like Zeke every time the sun came up.

She felt her ovaries shift. She was going to be twenty-nine soon; she was quickly moving through her fertile years. She didn't share this with anyone, but she wanted babies. Beautiful, chocolate brown ones that she could love on the way she'd always dreamed she would.

Addison glanced at the picture of Christopher again. She wasn't sure if it would happen. She hadn't met a decent, dateable man in years. She was done with the dating apps. She was done with other online dating sites. She was done with all of it. Jesus was going to have to drop a man from heaven. She'd put herself out there enough.

She put her phone down and glanced out the window. Two men got out of a pickup truck. Though they were wearing broad cowboy hats, she recognized Stone. Honestly, she'd know that butt anywhere. The man's body was sick.

She pursed her lips. That's why her eggs were rotting. Too many men were womanizing, serial-daters like Stone Bennett. The magazine had the nerve to be featuring him as an available bachelor. He was about as available as a man in prison.

She sighed and continued to watch as he and the man got on one of those golf carts and took off down the road leading further into the property. Addison frowned. Where was he going when he was supposed to be working with her?

"How is he going to work with you when you're barely out of bed?" She tapped her phone screen to check the time. It was a little before 8 a.m. She supposed things got going on the ranch early. Just then, the phone rang, and she answered Harper's video call.

Harper was an early riser. "Do you want to have lunch?"

"You're back?" Addison didn't recognize the background of the room Harper was in, but then she realized if she was back, she was at Logan's house, and she'd never seen the master bedroom there.

"I am. I came in late last night."

"Tearing yourself away from your groom so quickly? I thought you guys were staying a few more days."

"My beloved got called to Vegas to deal with some legal issues. This Vegas hotel continues to be drama. Anyway, Logan is optimistic that he can break ground."

"I'm surprised you didn't go to Vegas with him. You have been glued to each other for a month."

"Whew, chile, I need a break from Logan Bennett. My wifely ministry gots me wore out." She chuckled. "Plus, I have my period. He ain't ready for how I start acting."

Addison poked her lips out like a bothered three-year-old. "Do not mention your wifely ministry to someone in my situation. I am straight jealous."

"Sorry, girl. Anyway, if things go well in Vegas, I'll be joining next week. If not, I'm headed to New York for some meetings with my staff."

"Busy, busy, busy wife of a hotelier."

Harper rolled her neck. "I'm the VP of Architecture and Design for a chain of hotels. I just happened to be married to the owner. Acknowledge a sister."

Addison rolled her own neck. "Okay, you won't have to correct me again. I know you've been out here making your own moves for a long time."

"Good. Now that that's settled. You want to have lunch?"

"I am not in Forest Hills. I'm a little out of town." She raised her phone, pointed it out at the room and panned it so Harper could see the space.

"Somebody has nice taste. Where are you?"

"You're not going to believe this." She paused for dramatic effect. "Stone Bennett's house."

Harper frowned. "Stone? Explain yourself."

Addison filled her in on the details.

Harper laughed. "You've got to be kidding me."

"I'm not."

"Manipulative much?"

"Yeah. Too much."

"He's interested in you," Harper teased.

Addison shook her head. "He's interested in winning."

The smile dropped from Harper's face. "He does have a history that would indicate that."

Last night's romantic setting flittered through her mind in quick flashes. "He's smooth. I'll give him that."

"What's the rest of his place like?"

"Enormous. Just like him."

"Girrrl," Harper laughed. "I'm telling you, watch the millionaire magic. It can mess you up."

"I'm good. I know what it is with him."

Harper got up and moved out of frame before coming back with a tube of something and opening it. "How long are you going to be there?"

"Until this afternoon."

Harper smeared a clay mask on her face. "Well, a late dinner. I'll get takeout and come over."

"Sounds good," Addison agreed, and they ended the call.

She stood and went to the bathroom to take a shower. The sooner she got dressed, the sooner she could sit him down and get her questions answered. Lord knows, the last thing she wanted to do was hang out with Stone all day. She entered the room and noted the large, jetted, soaking tub and decided maybe she wouldn't get to that sit down as quickly as she thought she would.

Chapter 6

"There you go," Stone said, stepping back from the pony and handing the reins to one of the ranch hands. "Be easy with him, and he'll be easy with you."

The toothless, seven-year-old boy smiled at him and stuck out his chest as the pony trotted down the dirt path behind the others. The horse was being led by the ranch hand, but the boy was still excited he was riding. He glanced over his shoulder and said, "Thank you, Mr. Bennett."

Stone waved and watched as the group of twenty kids were led on their tour.

Stone's ranch manager, Josiah Henderson, known as Joe, was standing next to him. "Did the hats come in?" Stone asked.

"They arrived on Friday. All two thousand of them." Joe smiled, and both men turned and got on a golf cart.

"Good," Stone said, starting the cart and turning it in the direction of the main house. "I hate when kids leave without a hat."

Stone had opened limited number of visits to the ranch as a local attraction for school children. Tours were offered at no cost, so the schools and daycare centers flocked to the place as often as they could get a space. Stone liked sending each child away with their own personal cowboy hat.

"You know, no one would judge you if you charged $5 a person to offset the cost," Joe said. "You feed them lunch and breakfast, all the activities are free, and then they leave with a real hat."

Stone chuckled. "Giving away some of my money to kids does my heart good. I'll let you know when I stop earning interest on my fortune."

Joe nodded. "It's my job to keep this place liquid. You pay me more than anyone would for the pleasure."

"You know my vision, Joe." Stone glanced to his partner and friend. "I'm grooming the next generation of cowpokes."

Joe nodded. "So, this woman at the house, might she be the future Mrs. Bennett? The one to give you your own little cowpokes?"

Stone's reply was a frown.

"I'm just asking." Joe threw up his hands. "You never bring anyone to the house. I was shocked when you told me you had someone here."

cinnamon brown, homemade bread Swenson had on the counter. She was the only Ingram with light eyes. She'd gotten them from her father. She'd gotten her looks from her father period. He remembered meeting the man once during a family vacation. He took her hand, and whispered, "Neither."

Addison frowned. "Neither what?"

Stone was amused. She'd forgotten her own question. "I wasn't birthing a heifer, and I wasn't with a two-legged one. That is unless you're calling Joe names."

She pulled her hand from his and turned back to the island where she picked up her phone and a notebook. "Can we get to our business?"

"I've been rubbing up against horses all morning. I need to clean up first."

Addison lifted an eyebrow. "Aren't you always rubbing up against horses?"

"I don't have people around me when I do, except the ones who also smell like horses."

Addison continued to look annoyed.

"I promise, I'll answer your questions as soon as I get out of the shower."

She put the notebook down.

"Unless you want to join me."

Now she rolled her eyes. "Don't play."

"Just making sure you haven't changed your mind," he said. "Did Swenson show you the great room or something with a couch?"

"I figured if I hung out here, I would luck up on another meal like the one he served me this morning."

"I'll text him and ask him to serve lunch early. Come on," he said, rolling his head toward the door. "I've got the perfect spot for you."

Addison gathered her things and followed him into the hallway. Her suitcase stood out as an addition to the décor on the wall by the main entrance. She was indeed ready to leave him. He took her past several rooms to the back of the house where he had a sunroom. It was light and airy. His sister, Trinity, decorated it the last time she visited. In fact, she called it Trinity's room and told him she expected him to have sign made that said so by the time she came back to the states. He hadn't moved on that because she made no promises about when that would be.

Addison stepped in and he knew his sister had been right. Her mouth dropped open. He watched as she took in the white leather furniture and sheer window treatments. Original works of art included paintings of Black women, including a recreation of a photograph of his mother. The scent was of lavender and jasmine because fresh flowers were delivered to the room every other week.

"This is so different from the rest of the house. Feminine."

"Trinity decorated it. She said it would be the perfect space in the house for any woman looking for a quiet place to gather her thoughts."

Addison nodded agreeably. "She's right." She sat and put her phone and the long-handled bag she carried on the table in front of her. She pushed her back into the cushion and placed an arm on the end of the couch. Her long, curly hair was pulled up into a high ponytail. She was dressed in denim shorts with a white tee and a yellow linen blazer. The yellow complimented her honey complexion. Her long, glossy legs were an unnecessary distraction. As were her feet in the yellow straps of leather. More yellow adorned her toenails. She had pretty feet. But he'd known that because he'd seen them many times.

"Did you bring sneakers?" he asked. "This interview will include a tour of my ranch."

She looked put off, but not necessarily by him. It was more of a "why didn't I think of that?" kind of expression.

"I did," she replied.

"Change into them while you wait. I'll be fifteen minutes." He left the room and headed for his bedroom.

Stone made quick work of showering and changing into a fresh shirt and jeans before plopping down in the chair in front of the desk. He picked up a printout of the book cover he'd had designed.

We Were First: The Story of Black Cowboys by Stone Bennett and Arthur Shaw. He'd have to have the cover redone. Shaw and he had split ways last year when it was discovered the man plagiarized several of the books he'd ghostwritten. Stone was glad the story broke before Shaw had gotten too far into the project. The last thing he wanted was the legacy of Black cowboys to be tarnished by inauthentic scandal. People would already question the history because it included the truth that the first non-Mexican cowboys in this country were Black men.

He'd been looking for another writer—the right writer—someone he could trust completely. He was sure he'd found her. He just had to convince her the story mattered.

Stone went to his closet and removed another pair of cowboy boots from his collection of two hundred and pulled them on. He found Addison in the room, standing near the small library with a book in her hand.

"What's this?" she asked, showing it to him.

Stone stepped closer and noted it was a scrapbook he'd kept of the many pictures of Black cowboys going all the way back to the 1700's. He took it from her hand and placed it on the shelf she'd gotten it from.

"We'll talk about that later. Let's go so we can get back for lunch."

Chapter 7

By the time they'd toured Stone's enormous property, Addison was thanking God for Stone's foresight in telling her to change her footwear. He still hadn't answered her question about the scrapbook clippings in Trinity's room. He had enough pictures to make a coffee table book or even an exhibit of some kind in a museum.

She let it go and focused on the present experience. The ranch was breathtaking. She could tell by the many parts of the property that he took his business to raise and train horses seriously.

"This ranch..." he said, picking up where he'd left off in his detailed and practiced tour-guidish speech, "... is widely regarded as the historical birthplace of the finest Clydesdale horses in the country right now, if not the world. And it all started with one horse, Delonte. More than seventy percent of the stallions and mares on this property are descendants from that one horse my great-grandfather purchased in 1905."

Addison's mouth fell open. "That's remarkable. I'm speechless." She raised a hand to her forehead to block the sunlight hovering above. "How many horses do you have?"

Stone parked the golf cart in front of a building marked Bennett Stables and offered her a hand to help her step down.

"I have fifteen horses of my own that I ride and keep around for family and friends for visits, but as a part of the business, there are over four hundred on the property right now."

Her mouth dropped open again. She knew she'd seen a good hundred in the area he called the East Corral and the same in the South Corral.

"Four hundred horses. What about the cattle?"

Stone laughed. "I have a few way down on the west end. They are a part of the farm we have on the property, but I don't raise cattle."

"Why did you laugh?"

"It's a common stereotype. Ranches and cattle."

"Do you enter any of your horses in the rodeo?"

Stone stepped into the stable and she followed him. The smell of horses and hay was pungent, but not unpleasant. She was glad it didn't stink of manure.

Stone walked up to a stall and raised his hand to pet the horse inside. It was a beautiful, tall, shiny black horse. "Not all horses want to go to the rodeo."

One of his employees walked out of stall and toward them. He tipped his hat to her. "Ma'am." Then he asked Stone, "Did you want to take her out today?"

Stone nodded and raised two fingers to the man. Addison watched as he reached for a saddle from the hook against the wall.

"There are different kinds of cowboys, Addy. Some ride only, others get out and rope, some rodeo as bull riders, some do raise cattle, and then others like me...I raise horses to sell and for some equestrian sport."

Addison was recording, because he let her today, but some things, she wrote down because it was just her habit to do so. "Explain the sport part."

Stone took her hand and pulled her back. She'd been so busy writing, she hadn't noticed the enormous animal was being led out of the barn.

"People come here to learn to ride."

Addison was surprised. She thought Stone was a private person, that all this land was just for him and the animals and other cow persons, not other people.

"This..." he said, gently tugging on the horse's neck gear, "...is March. She is one of the most famous American Quarter horses in the U.S. She's won quite a few show ribbons in her life too."

"So you race her?"

"Not anymore. She's a show horse now. I race my thoroughbreds. That's a whole 'nother breed. I'll show you." He extended a hand to her.

Addison stared in disbelief. "You want me to ride her?"

"We are going to ride her."

Addison hesitated. She'd ridden a horse before, but it never occurred to her he'd want her to ride today.

He continued to hold his hand out. "She's a good girl. I promise."

Addison slipped her phone in the pocket of her crossbody bag. Stone guided her to the stirrup and supported her as she got up. Then he climbed on himself. Even though the saddle was divided with hump in the middle, they were close. She was pressed against his back, and she had no choice but to put her arms around his waist to hold on. The man had a stomach made of pure muscle. She turned her head to the side and released the long breath she'd been holding since she'd had to touch him.

Stone pulled on the reins and guided the horse down the incline and onto the road. Addison felt dizzy for a moment. She didn't realize how tall the horse was or how long its legs were until it moved downward. She squeezed Stone's belly.

He careened his neck in her direction. "You okay?"

Realizing he could feel the tension in her body, she released her grip some and muttered. "Mmhmm."

"You've ridden before?" he asked.

"I have," she said.

"I don't want you to feel sick."

"No, I…" she didn't know what to say. She didn't want to admit she hadn't been this close to a man in two years. She hadn't inhaled the smell of sandalwood soap coming off a man's freshly showered skin, or the scent of the shampoo he'd used. She couldn't quite put her name to that smell, maybe more cedar. It was woodsy and warm, but sweet at the same time. He smelled rugged, masculine, fresh, and if tough was a scent, he had it. "I'm fine. It has been a while."

Stone pulled on the reins and sped the horse up a bit. As he'd done in the golf cart, he gave her a guided tour of everything they were passing. As they approached the corral, a school bus pulled out of a small parking lot to the left of the building and moved onto the main road.

"What's that?" Addison asked, squinting. "It looks like kids."

"It is," he said. "I allow some local tours from the schools and daycare centers."

The horse galloped to a trough and like lightening, Stone climbed down from the horse and reached for her hand.

"You're fast," she said.

He lowered her slowly. Much slower than he had to as her face came within inches of his. Their eyes locked as he held her suspended. His dropped to her lips. Hers rose to his and then they both raised them and locked on each other's gazes. They were too close. She was even closer to him than he had been on the horse.

"Put me down," she whispered.

Stone's expression was cocky and sure, but he placed her on her feet. Unexpectedly, a tug of friendship or something else pulled between them. Resisting the feeling, Addison stepped back.

Stone didn't move. His eyes traveled the length of her like that slight press against her body had awakened something in him.

She cleared her throat and hoped it would clear his mind. "I don't have all day."

He looked at his watch. "We'll go back for lunch in a minute. I felt your stomach growling. I thought you were going to eat my back." He tied the horse to a pole.

She was glad he broke the intensity between them with the teasing.

Stone took her inside the stable and showed her his prized thoroughbreds and two of the most beautiful horses she'd ever seen—an Arabian and an Akhal-Teke.

"These horses probably cost more than I'll ever earn."

Stone frowned. "Don't downplay your potential, Addy. You're young."

She cocked her head. "I feel the money."

Stone laughed. "Together they cost close to ten million dollars."

Her mouth dropped open again. She couldn't even speak this time.

"They're an investment. They'd sell for more, but I'd never sell them." He rubbed the coat of the blonde Akhal-Teke.

He walked away and had a conversation further down the stable with one of his employees. Addison removed her cell phone, turned off the flash and took a few pictures of the horses. Stone returned to her side.

"I know you're scheduled for a photo shoot, but do you mind me taking a shot of you with your horses? Who knows, the resolution might be strong enough for the feature."

Stone obliged her, then said, "Let's go. You're hungry and so am I."

They rode back to the stable and then took the golf cart to the house.

A full buffet was prepared for them. Several of Stone's staff were seated and eating.

After she fixed her plate with fried chicken, cold cuts, homestyle potato salad, baked beans, a few rolls and chow-chow, Stone took it from her hands.

Whispering, he said, "Follow me. I have a private spot."

He led her to the outside deck. Stone kicked a plate just inside the door and they walked out.

"What was that?" she asked, looking down.

"A cooling unit. It's kind of like outside AC."

Addison nodded and followed him to the table. The things Stone's kind of money could buy. Ten-million-dollar horses, outside AC...did it ever end? She sat and accepted her plate from him. He stood and walked to a serving table near where they'd entered and poured two glasses of lemonade and brought them to the table.

"Thank you," Addison said. She looked at the beautiful bouquet of fresh cut flowers in the center of the table and noticed a card on them. Her name was written on it.

Stone blushed a little and said, "They're yours." He closed his eyes and said a private grace. So did she. After, she reached for the card, opened it, and read:

Addison,

I hope this interview was more pleasant than you expected.

~Stone

She looked at him. Her heart did what it had been doing since last night—sped up like a lovesick teenager. She needed it to stop doing that. This was Stone Bennett. She looked at him. She noticed the one dimple on the left side of his face. She'd spent so much time avoiding Stone—not seeing him—that she'd forgotten the indentation in his cheek. His toffee complexion gleamed under the sun. His neat goatee framed his dentist office smile. He was good looking. Very. Those Bennett genes were fire anyway, and this man had more than his fair share of the DNA.

She cleared her throat and placed the card down. "Thank you. You might have waited until I published the article. What if you don't like what I write?"

Stone dropped his eyes to his plate and inhaled a forkful of potato salad. He looked back up at her and said, "For some reason, I trust you." He wasn't smiling when he said it; there was no hint of humor in his voice. It was almost like he struggled to get the words out. And in his eyes, she saw something flash that warned her he was not a man who trusted often.

"I've seen your ranch. Most or some of it. Certainly, enough of it. But now you need you to answer my questions about you."

"My stomach's empty." His teasing smile was back.

Addison laughed at herself for walking into that. "How did I know you were going to say that?"

"Because I'm simple and predictable. I told you last night. I'm not that interesting."

Did he really believe that? Addison couldn't imagine he did because he was the opposite of uninteresting. She bit her lip and reached for her glass. Looking away, she took a sip and tried to avoid his stares as she ate.

Just as they finished eating, her phone buzzed with the signal for emergency alerts. She reached in and read it.

"The weather is going to be bad this evening in northwest Atlanta. Thunderstorms and a possible tornado."

Stone pitched an eyebrow. "That's in your path home."

She removed the pen and pad from her bag and said, "Let's get this done so I can get on the road before it begins."

Stone's phone rang. He raised a finger, signaling her to give him a moment. He answered, but she could tell there was no one on the other end. He ended the call and dialed to make a call, but didn't get an answer. "We have signal problems up here sometimes. Someone is trying to reach me." He stood and gathered their dishes and walked them to the buffet server. "Let's go in. The sun is high. I don't want you to get burned."

Addison followed him through the door and then she remembered her flowers and went back for them. It had been a long time since someone gave her flowers. Receiving them was a little off-putting, but nice, even if it was a work gift.

Once inside, they went to the great room and sat. Stone stepped across the room to try his call again. While he was waiting, Swenson arrived with two fresh glasses of lemonade. "Unless you'd like tea or a soft drink, ma'am."

"No, the lemonade is perfect."

He left it and walked away. Addison wondered if the man had a tracking device on Stone. He appeared to anticipate all his moves and showed up with whatever was needed.

Stone returned to the couch. "I am expecting a call back that I have to take. I don't want you to think I'm being rude, but it can't wait."

Addison nodded. "Then let's get what we can do done." She flipped open a notebook. "I already know you live here in Mountainville, grew up in Houston, but then moved to Forest Hills as a teenager."

"Piney Point Village. It's a suburb of Houston," he said, correcting her.

"College at?"

"Yale."

"Really?"

"And I actually graduated with honors."

"This is off the record. What was your major?"

"Business management. I knew I wanted to own a ranch."

"Hmph," escaped her lips. "Something people would never guess about you?"

"I'm an Internet-ordained minister."

Addison laughed. "What?"

"I had a buddy decide he was getting married. He was leaving for the military, and they couldn't find a reverend to do a quickie wedding, so I went online and got certified."

"That's hilarious."

He shrugged. "Next invasive and embarrassing question."

"Who are the people who inspire you most?"

"Cole. He's been through a lot, but his faith has always stayed strong. He impresses me daily."

"Person, dead or alive, you would want to meet most?"

"That's easy. Bill Pickett."

"The great Black Cowboy." She noted and Stone nodded. "What's the best advice you've ever received?"

He rolled his eyes up for a second and then answered quickly. "Use things, not people."

"What can't you get enough of?"

"Barbecue."

Addison nodded. She liked barbecue too. "Something you do every day, no matter what."

He took a deep breath and pushed his back further into the cushion. "Pray and read my Bible."

Addison looked curious. "Really?"

"I'm a devout Christian."

"Who runs through women."

"I don't run through women. I date, often because I'm a single, red-blooded man who's not married…hence this dumb interview."

Addison fought sighing. She wasn't going to argue with this carnal behind man. She dropped her eyes to her notes. "Okay, I'll get back to the script."

Stone leaned forward, reached for his drink, and took a sip. Smiling, he said, "You do that."

"Biggest turn-on?"

"A woman who smiles."

A smile slipped onto Addison's mouth before she could stop it.

"Just like that," he said huskily.

She blushed red and cleared her throat before the next question. "You know you're in love when?"

He inhaled deep and exhaled, avoided her eyes when he said, "I haven't been in love."

"Never?"

He twisted his lips. "Not that I recall."

She didn't believe him. "Not in elementary school or high school or college?"

"Nope."

Addison could tell the answer to that question was not "nope" because she saw a flash of pain cross his face, but she wasn't going to push it. This was not investigative journalism. It was entertainment. "I need to record an answer, so what might you do if you were in love?"

He shrugged. "I don't know. Maybe set an alarm on a Saturday morning so I can make her breakfast before she wakes up."

Addison bit her lip as a vision of that came to mind. "That's a good answer."

He cleared his throat and sat back again. "Next question."

"What, sir, is the key to your heart?" Addison had been writing, but she looked up at him. "Make it up if you have to."

He licked his lips and picked at the leather of the couch like he was trying to pull lint. Then he rattled off a list. "Kindness, intelligence, an adventurous spirit, a sense of humor. I need belly laughs in my life and," he hesitated. "... a genuine love for God. She'll need it to deal with me."

His phone rang. He leaned forward and picked it up. "This is my call." He stood and walked to the windows.

Addison raised her notebook and briefly fanned herself. It wasn't hot in the house, but it was warm in this room. If he meant them, those were some sweet and sexy answers. Whomever would eventually steal his heart was going to be one lucky woman.

"That's done," Stone said, putting his phone down. He stretched his arms across the back of the couch again and said, "I promise no more interruptions. I'm all yours."

Addison felt that tug between them again. She had to fight to focus, because it hadn't been twenty-four hours since she'd been with him, and every impression she had of Stone Bennett had shifted. He was a bed-hopping bachelor to be sure, but he was a nice one.

Chapter 8

When Addison dropped her notebook on the table, Stone's suspicion that she hated doing this interview was confirmed. He didn't think it had anything to do with him. It was the story. It included silly, trite questions that were beneath someone as intelligent as Addison.

"You look frustrated."

She hiked a shoulder. "It doesn't have anything to do with you."

"Not interested in the bachelors of Atlanta?"

She smirked. "Not in the least." She picked up her lemonade and finished the glass. "Don't tell Tom I complained." Her phone alert for the emergency notifications sounded again, and she looked at it.

"How long is the warning?"

She sighed. "Seven p.m. The weather is moving east and covers the area from Dawson to South Fulton County."

Stone frowned. "You're stuck with me."

Addison stood. "Not really. If I go now, I can beat it."

"If you leave now, you could get caught in it."

She picked up her bag. "I'll be fine."

Stone stood too. "You're not driving into a potential tornado."

"I don't like to drive at night."

"So, stay, Addy. It's not like someone else has your room for tonight."

She hesitated. She reached up and twirled a finger around a clump of her curly hair. "I'm ready to go home."

Stone stepped closer. "Ready to go home or ready to get away from me?"

She tilted her head up at him. "Maybe both."

He examined her face for a moment. The sharp, but feminine lines of it. He wanted to raise his hand and outline it with a finger. Her chin was particularly tempting. It looked kissable, as did her lips. "Am I so bad?"

Addison's face filled with heat. She dropped her head and stepped back.

He continued. "Haven't I been on my best behavior?"

"I just don't think there's anything to be worried about. We get warnings all the time. People still move about in the city." She said the words on shaky breath, but it wasn't the storm that had her nervous. He was right. It was him. She was feeling the same thing he was feeling.

"Well," he paused and spoke gently as to soften the impact of what he was about to say. "You're not people who have to move about. And I've got your keys. I'm not letting you drive into a storm."

This time when her face turned red, it was anger. "You can't hold my keys."

"I can, and I will. To protect you."

She put a hand on her hip. "You're not serious."

He shrugged. "I am completely serious."

She dropped her head for a moment, raised it and said, "I don't believe you would do such a thing, but I will use good sense and stay."

He nodded. Relief and excitement coursed through his veins. He was glad to have another night with her.

"I'll go back to my room and get some writing done."

"You can do that or use Trinity's room or if you prefer," he walked past her and waved her to follow him to the area where there were offices. He opened a door. "You can use this room. It's the library. I assume you like to read, and the chair is comfortable. You've got a great view of the ranch. I'm across the hall. So is Joe. The Wi-Fi is strong and reliable in this area."

He pushed a switch on the panel next to him and the huge picture that was in the center of a far wall began displaying digital images of famous places around the world. "There's a remote on the desk. You can choose to view works of art or even my collection of Bennett photographs."

He was selling it too hard. His desire to have her stay closer than her bedroom was overwhelming and silly, yet here he was…practically begging.

Addison inspected the room. "This is nice. Thank you."

Stone stuck his hands in his pockets. "The Wi-Fi password is on the desk blotter."

She nodded.

"I'll go," he said. He took his hands out of his pockets. She had him acting all jittery and unsure of himself. "Door open or closed?"

She hesitated before saying, "Closed."

He left her.

***

Stone spent a few hours working on the plan for his annual youth camp. He usually did most of this work with his staff in early June at a two-day planning retreat, but he decided to delve in and was glad for the distraction from Addison. He'd been working for almost three hours. He looked at his watch. It was dinnertime. He stood, stretched, and left the office.

He hung outside the library for a minute. The temptation to invite her to dinner was strong, but he'd promised to leave her alone, so he headed for the kitchen by himself.

Swenson was there, pulling a lasagna out of the oven. His semi-retired chef only came a few days a week. He prepared several meals and left them in the fridge and freezer.

"Will Miss Ingram be joining you?"

Stone washed his hands. "I don't know."

"She's a spirited young woman."

Stone picked a cherry tomato out of a bowl on the counter. "Yes, she is."

"Her bed has been slept in… as has yours."

Stone shot him a careful warning. "That's none of your business."

"The devil it isn't. You need to settle down. She might be just the one to make you."

"Why would you think I'd want to settle down?"

"She's unnerved you. You've been jumpy since you met with her the other night. That's not like you. Not at all. And you brought her here—I suspect for a reason."

"I need dinner." Stone stuck the tomato and then another in his mouth. "Go on with your nosy self. I can fix my own food."

Swenson laughed. He removed a bowl of salad and dressing from the refrigerator. He put two sets of dinnerware and silverware on the table. "Suit yourself. Let me know if Miss Ingram doesn't come in for dinner. I'll take something to her." He left the kitchen and then stuck his head back in and clapped twice before saying, "Dinner music."

Stone shook his head and grabbed a beer from the refrigerator. He questioned his decision not to get Addison, but decided it was best to let her be before he had to hog tie her to keep her from talking about leaving again. He groaned against the idea of eating alone when her charming personality was in the house, but he sat and fixed a plate of salad. Just as he was about to stick his fork in, Addison entered the kitchen. He knew it was a corny thing to think, but the room brightened with her entrance.

He couldn't keep the smile off his face. "You're just in time. It's hot out of the oven."

"Good. I'm starving." She sat and fixed a plate. "I thought you didn't like salad."

Stone shoved it aside like she'd reminded him of the fact. "It's Italian food. A little is required, right?" He took a sip of his beer. "Anyway, the lasagna is amazing. I had it at a dinner party and then stole the chef from the family he was working for."

She shook her head. "Such a millionaire move."

"What's money good for if you can't flex sometimes?"

"The way you flexed to get me here?" She pinned him with a look for a moment.

He smiled and raised his beer bottle to his lips. "Guilty," he said. He didn't feel guilty at all and she looked like she knew it. Little attitude and all, it was good to be sitting across from her. "Did you get some work done?"

"A little. What about you?"

"A lot."

Addison chewed some and then spoke again. "What does a cowboy do in his office?"

"A lot actually, but Joe handles most of it. I was working on an event I sponsor."

"What kind?"

"It's just a…thing. Nothing worth getting into." He waved the question away. He hadn't meant to bring it up. "I found that story I was telling you about. The one that made me want to be a cowboy. It's on my desk. I'll show it to you later."

Other than the clink of silverware on their plates, the only sound in the room was the music Swenson started. Stone wasn't sure what he was supposed to do. Did she want to talk or no? Then he realized he was being silly. She was just a woman. He was good with women. "I never asked. When is the article you're writing coming out?"

"It's the July issue. It'll be out at the end of June. It's the Summer Love edition."

He nodded. "Perfect. I can expect to get many, many DMs and some good old-fashioned, love letters."

"More than the usual. Possibly accompanied by nude pics and panties in the mail."

He huffed. "I already get those."

"And who has the honor of tossing the underwear in the trash?"

"Swenson. He's really good at it."

Addison's full lips curved into a smile. He couldn't help but think about how sweet they must be. Why didn't the only woman he wanted right now want him?

"Stone, did you hear me?"

He tilted his head and squinted. He had not.

"I asked you if you ever miss Forest Hills?"

"When I do, I visit."

"Not often, or at least I guess I don't hear about you visiting often."

"I don't miss it much."

"I can see why. It's beautiful here. Your people seem like family." Addison stabbed a piece of lettuce and stuck it in her mouth. After she chewed and swallowed, she asked, "Do you have friends?"

"A few. I get invited to dinner all the time. Everyone wants to see me get married, preferably to their daughter."

"Well, at least it's not to their sons."

He chuckled. "Not yet." Stone said, serving the lasagna. "Have you ever thought about leaving Forest Hills?"

"I did. I went to college in New York, but I missed Atlanta. It's home. I'd miss my sisters."

"I understand that."

"Cole seems happy with Lenise."

"Yes, you helped with that."

"All I did was get some tickets and help him with some plans." Their eyes caught for a moment again. She broke the stare. "Your brother surprised me. He's been pretty unattached."

"You know what they say. The right woman can get any man to settle down." He gave her a half smile. She returned her attention to her plate.

"Do you always eat in here?"

"Yeah, the dining room is a little lonely. I save it for guests." He cleared his throat. "I eat most days with my staff."

"And today?"

"They know you're here, so they won't come up to the house."

She raised a napkin and wiped her mouth. Wrinkles lined her forehead. "I don't want to deprive them of a good lasagna."

"Swenson took care of them. Chef always makes three."

"That's generous." She took a few bites of salad before raising her beautiful eyes to meet his again. "How many people live on the property?"

"Sixteen. That includes seven cowboys and three cowgirls. I've got three married couples mixed in there." He took a sip of water and returned his glass to the table before finishing. "Then there's security. I have a small team. Swenson lives here and two maids."

The ate in silence for a few minutes, pausing and locking eyes before returning to their respective plates. Addison was always the first one to look away. She seemed nervous around him, nearly coy, and he liked it. His gut told him she was fighting attraction. He was never wrong about that.

Desperately wanting the answer to not be lock herself away, he asked, "So what are your plans for the evening?"

Three raps on the exterior door interrupted them. His people knew to come in if no one answered, so he waited until he saw the visitor enter. It was Bones, one of the supervisors.

Stone stood. "Bones, this is Miss Addison Ingram. Addison, this is Bones. He manages the East Corral. He was out earlier today when we stopped by."

Bones removed his hat, and they greeted each other.

"So, what's up?" Stone already knew it had to be important for Bones to come to the house like this. Word had spread that he had a woman here that wasn't a Bennett. That was a big deal.

"I don't mean to disturb you, but you said you wanted to know when Hessy went into labor, sir. We called Doc."

Stone nodded.

"I tried your cell."

"I left it in my office. I'll be right over."

Bones put his hat back on and left. Stone returned to the table. He finished a few more forkfuls of lasagna and downed a glass of water. "Have a snack with me later?"

Addison nodded. He stood, touched her shoulder, and then raised his hand to her chin and tipped it up. "Don't hesitate to let Swenson know if you need something. He's underutilized, overpaid, and likes to feel important."

Addison smiled. It was nice having her here. She felt like she belonged to him. Every cell in his body was begging him to kiss her—even if it was just on the forehead, but he resisted. He didn't want to scare her away. "Don't eat all the pie," he teased.

Her smiled widened. His heart swelled, and he left the house to join Bones.

Chapter 9

Addison stood and went to the window. She watched Stone get on a golf cart and ride down the mile-long path until he disappeared. She raised a hand to touch her lips. She thought he was going to kiss her. Oddly, she'd wanted him to. Being alone with him felt comfortable. He was starting to feel like a friend. She'd known Stone since she was a child, but she'd never thought of him as a friend. He had such a reputation. The last thing she needed in her life was a player. She'd had enough of that already, but friends, one could never have too many of them.

Addison returned to the table and finished her dinner. She was just about to wash their dishes when the maid entered.

"Oh no, ma'am. I'll take care of it." The woman practically begged her not to deal with the dishes. She respected the order of things and excused herself.

"Back to the work I go," she whispered as she walked down the long corridor that led to the library. She opened her notes she had on the story she was pecking away at about Georgia's charter schools. But Addison couldn't keep her mind on her work, so she examined the room.

Stone's library was a handsome room with heavy brown woods trimmed with beige and cream. The books were leather bound, mostly classics that she wondered if he'd read. She was used to working at her cubicle or her office at home. Both were light and airy spaces decorated with yellow sunflowers and pineapples. She'd pinned an emoji she'd made from a yellow paper plate on the back of her laptop every day to let her coworkers know what kind of mood to expect from her. Most of the time it was a happy face emoji, but sometimes it was sad or tense or plain old angry. People thought it was cute. She was keeping it real.

She wasn't used to working somewhere so elegant, so she continued to be distracted. She knew her unfamiliar surroundings were mostly to blame, but the other problem was she was distracted by the stable in the distance. She was thinking about Stone and the horse and wondering how long it took for a horse to deliver a baby. Was it like human childbirth? Was there a range? She Googled it.

"Anywhere from two to about six hours for a mare to go through all three stages of labor," she read aloud. He'd been gone for less than two. But he'd asked her to wait on dessert, so maybe he wasn't expecting it to take long. Addison closed her laptop. She had given up on her muse when she remembered Stone told her he'd left the story that inspired his cowboy fascination on his desk. She popped up, stretched, and walked across the hall to his office. She walked around the desk and found an old story about a cowboy. His name was Wes Bennett. He'd died in the year 1938, so before Stone's grandfather was even born. She figured he had to be his great-grandfather or some relative.

She read the story and just as she stood to leave, she noticed a bunch of printouts with pie charts and graphs and then some handwritten notes and mind mapping diagrams. She meant to only peek, but by the time she finished looking, she discovered Stone was planning a summer camp for kids from Atlanta. She also discovered he'd been having the camp for years. It was the North Georgia Cowboy Camp.

"Interesting," she mused. "You have a secret passion, Stone Bennett."

She left his office and went back to the library, opened her laptop with new interest. After Googling, she found several articles and lots of pictures about the camp. Very few of the pictures included Stone.

She saved the articles to her Stone file on the server. Then she shut down her laptop, grabbed her phone, and went outside to the deck. It was a little chilly as it often was in the mountains in early summer, but not bad enough to send her back in the house. The night sky captured and held her attention. The low hanging stars were enigmatic lights, creeping across the sky through a film of clouds. She recognized constellations, took her time picking them out and taking a few pictures. She also photographed the grounds. This view. It was worth every penny Stone paid for it.

"The things money buys," she whispered. Heaven on earth. She was glad she'd stayed an extra night to see it. Speaking of which, she'd forgotten Harper was expecting her for a late dinner. She removed her phone and noted she'd missed two text messages from her. Stone was right. The signals out here weren't great. She dialed Harper's number.

"Are you off the road? The weather is wicked."

"I'm still here. I'm staying an extra night."

"Well, you could have told me. I've been a little worried that you were coming down I-75 tonight."

"I'm sorry. I went down a research hole and lost track of time."

"You're still working?"

"I was. I'm just hanging out now. Stone is delivering a baby horse tonight."

"Oh, how interesting. I'm surprised you aren't with him."

"He didn't invite me. Plus it takes a long time. He probably didn't think I'd want to be in a stable that long."

"You'd smell like a horse for sure," Harper said. "I'm on with Logan, so let me click back. I'm glad to know you stayed put."

They ended the call.

Addison looked at the time and once again wondered how late Stone would be with the birth. She noticed there was a golf cart parked in the covered area adjacent to the garages. Hoping the keys were in the ignition, she went down the steps and walked over to it. She wanted to get a closer look at the lake. She could see the tail end of it in the distance. She climbed inside. Keys hung on a little hook overhead. She smiled, started it, and turned in the direction of the paved path to the lake.

Once she arrived, she saw a couple sitting on one of the benches. Cowboy and his cowgirl. *A cow couple*, she thought humorously. She remembered Stone told her he had two married couples working for him. The man stood, waving, and walked into her path. She slowed down and hit the brake once she was close enough to speak to him.

"Hello, Miss Addison." She recognized the man, but didn't recall his name. "Where are you headed?"

"I wanted to take in some air. See the lake."

He raised his hand in the direction of his wife. "Did you want to join us?"

"Oh, no. Three has always been a crowd. I'll go to the corral. Stone is delivering a baby."

"I heard. Do you want me to take you?"

Addison glanced at his waiting wife. "No. I'm fine. It's just down and to the left on the road."

"Second left and a right," he corrected her. He stepped closer. "Are you sure you don't want me to drop you off? It can get confusing at night."

"No. I'll be fine. The east was the first one we visited today. It's fresh in my mind."

He looked like he didn't want her to go alone, but he stepped back.

"Have a good evening." Addison hit the gas and inched the vehicle forward and then gunned it more to get back to the speed she'd been driving. Her phone rang and she reached into her pocket for it.

Lauren. She'd been trying to reach her for days. She answered.

"Hey, I've been trying to reach you."

"I know. Sorry, I've been dead tired at the end of the day. What's this I hear about you being at Stone's ranch?"

"It's a story for work."

"About Stone?"

Addison filled her in on the details. It ended with Lauren laughing. "What a silly thing to have to write."

"Don't laugh at me. I'm just trying to work my way up."

"If Beth doesn't do better by you, you need to quit."

"And do what?"

"Freelance. The money is good."

"I know, but it's not like taking pictures."

"Don't talk yourself out of what you can do. You're staying in Rachel's house. Your car is paid for. If you're going to branch out, this is the time."

A large animal scooted across the road in front of her. Addison screamed and slammed on the brakes. Her phone flew out of her hand. She could hear Lauren calling her name, but she was busy looking around for the offending creature. When she didn't see anything, she reached over and picked up the phone.

"I think I just saw a possum the size of a rottweiler."

"Yuk. What are you doing?"

She rubbed her hands up and down her arms. It had gotten chillier and windy. "I'm going to watch Stone deliver a baby horse."

Lauren didn't reply. She looked at the phone and realized the call had dropped. She put the phone on the empty seat next to her. She was going to have to turn soon, so she needed to pay attention.

She passed a road and when she came to the second one, she turned left. She rode for a while and then saw a building in the distance to the right, so she turned and headed that way. She pulled up to it. There was no light and no cars. She realized it wasn't the corral she was looking for. It didn't appear to be anything but an abandoned building. The first droplets of rain fell and hit the windshield, making popping sounds and leaving nickel size splotches behind.

She remembered her instructions—left on the second road. It had to be close, but it had gotten dark. She couldn't see far, and the trees were thick. The rain wasn't helping. Now she realized why the man wanted to drive her. This place was huge. It was easy to get lost.

"Why am I in the woods on a ranch in north Georgia in the dark?"

Addison reached for her phone. She needed to call Stone. She swiped and realized she didn't have a good signal, nor did she have Stone's telephone number. She'd never asked him for it. She called Rachel. She would have it and if she didn't, Zeke would give it to her. When Rachel answered, the call dropped immediately. She looked at the phone and her signal was completely gone.

Addison took a deep breath, backed up and turned the cart in the direction she'd come. She only made two turns or was it three or four? She drove for a few minutes before the cart slowed down, sputtered, and came to a stop.

She turned the flashlight on her phone and looked at the gauges.

GAS.

Empty.

Jesus.

***

Stone entered the house. He took off his boots and went to his bedroom where he showered and changed into a pair of jeans and a hoodie before going back to the kitchen. He noticed the key lime pie was in the fridge. Addison hadn't cut it. He hoped it was because she was waiting to share it with him. He went to the office area, peeked in where he left her. She wasn't there. He went to the TV room. She wasn't there. He headed to the Trinity room, but before he could get there, he saw it was dark. He called out, "Addison?"

Nothing came back to him. The house was silent. He checked the time on his phone. Nine thirty. She wouldn't be in bed, but she might be in her room. He went to the door and stood outside of it, hesitating about knocking. He'd promised her privacy, but he knocked anyway. This was his house.

She didn't answer. He knocked again. She still didn't answer. He pushed the door open and noted it was dark. The bed was made. The bathroom was dark. Her suitcase was here, expected since he had her keys. Still, he called her name and waited. When she didn't answer, he went deeper into the room and looked for her. She definitely wasn't here, and his gut told him something was wrong.

Stone went back to center of the foyer and yelled her name a few times. He took out his cell. He didn't have her number. He called Zeke.

"Hey, cuz."

"Hey, I need Addison's telephone number."

Zeke laughed. "I'm sure you do."

"No, seriously, she's here on the ranch. I can't find her. I have her car keys. I need to find her."

He could hear Rachel questioning him in the background. She came on the phone.

"What do you mean you can't find her?"

Stone raised a hand to his head. Frustrated, he ran his fingers over his hair. "I mean I don't know where she is, and I'm a little concerned about where she might have wandered off to."

"She tried to call me about forty minutes ago, but the call dropped."

"I need her number, Rachel."

Rachel gave it to him. He promised to have Addison call as soon as he located her. He called the number a few times, but it went to voicemail. He cursed under his breath.

Swenson came from the door that led to the servants' quarters. Stone filled him in.

"I haven't seen her since shortly after dinner," Swenson said. He offered to continue to help with checking the house in case she'd had an accident. Stone went out on the deck. He stood there for a minute under the falling rain and looked to his right. He realized one of the golf carts was missing.

He called security. When he got an answer, he said, "I'm looking for Miss Ingram. Did she leave?"

"No, sir."

"She's not in the house. I need you to call all staff to look for her. I think she's out on the property. One of the carts is missing." He groaned. What was she thinking? "I'll turn on my walkie-talkie."

"Yes, sir. I'll turn the lights on."

Before Stone could get in his truck, bright lights flooded the property. They only used them for extreme emergencies because the lights frightened the animals. He reached into the glove compartment and removed a walkie-talkie and turned it on. He headed down the road.

"Where are you, Addison?" he asked the question over and over, and prayed she would appear. The rain was coming down hard and the wind had picked up. The storm from further south had sent some of its nasty weather north.

Shortly into his ride, he got a call from the security officer. He advised she'd been seen over an hour ago, heading to the East Corral. Stone went that way. Addison was not there. He clenched his teeth, hating the thought of her being lost out here in the rain in a golf cart, probably with no phone signal.

Although it wasn't noticeable except on a map, the property was a rectangle. The roads were laid out in a grid. It was easy to get around when you knew the land, but of course, Addison did not. He couldn't imagine what made her think it was okay to drive out here.

It took another ten minutes for him to get his question answered. He found her sitting in the cart, wet, and shaking from the cold. He could surmise all that from his headlights. He got out of the truck. She got out of the cart. He ran toward her. She staggered toward him and into his arms. He picked her up and carried her to the truck. Once she was tucked in the seat, he removed his hoodie and pulled it over her head. Teeth chattering, she was more than happy to cooperate with his clumsy maneuvers around her body. He pushed the button to the turn the heat on full and gunned the engine to go back to the house. The walkie-talkie cracked and he answered, letting security know he'd found her. He told them to alert Swenson as well, then he put the walkie-talkie down.

"I could have used one of those," she said, teeth clicking on every word.

"Lost?"

"And out of gas."

"What were you thinking going off on your own like that?"

"I thought it would be interesting to see the baby horse be born."

He shook his head. "It never occurred to me that you'd want to see that."

She didn't respond. He glanced at her. Even with the heat on high, she was still shuddering. Stone took her hand and squeezed it. "Just a few more minutes. You can get out of those clothes, and we'll get you something warm to drink."

She squeezed his hand back and slid closer to him, seeking out his warmth.

One of the security team was standing at the garage when Stone pulled up. Stone stopped the truck, hopped out and lifted Addison off the seat.

"Put the truck up for me," he said before entering the house. He carried Addison to her bedroom and let her down. She reached for his t-shirt with both hands, clenching her fists around the fabric; she pushed her wet head into his chest. Stone wrapped his arms around her and pulled her deeper into him. Instinctively, he kissed the top of her head. It felt like something she needed; or maybe he was lying to himself. Maybe he was the one who needed it. Fear created adrenaline and that was a lot to come down from.

"You scared me to death," he whispered into her hair and inhaled a scent he loved. Coconut. "I don't think I've ever been that scared in my life." He squeezed her tighter and they stood there for a few moments with him holding her and her clinging to him. Finally, her teeth stopped chattering. She loosened the grip on his shirt and backed up.

"There are animals out there."

"Yeah, it's woods, sweetheart," he replied. "Real ones."

"I thought I was going to get eaten." She stepped back some more. "I should have known I'd gone too far when the trees got thicker."

He stepped to her, grabbed her hand, and pulled her back to him, enclosing her in his arms again. She felt good there. "It doesn't matter. You're safe. It's never going to happen again." He kissed the top of her head again.

Addison looked up at him. He thought he saw some relief in those beautiful eyes, but he also saw fatigue. Still, Stone didn't think he'd ever wanted to kiss a woman so badly. His adrenaline was still pumped from the search. "You need to get out of those wet clothes. I'm going to get you something hot."

She nodded. "Tea would be nice." She took a few steps backward, reached for the hem of his hoodie and pulled it over her head before handing it to him. "And pie." Finally, a smile broke through.

Stone smiled with her. "Next time you tell Swenson or security if you want to go somewhere."

She kicked off her shoes. "You don't have to warn me again."

"Did you want me to bring the drink up here, or did you want to come down?"

She rubbed her hands up and down her arms. "Up here would be nice."

Stone backed out of the room and went downstairs. He found Swenson in the kitchen, a steaming kettle on the stove.

"As usual, you guessed correctly. She would like a cup of tea." Stone washed his hands and cut two large pieces of pie.

Swenson put a carafe of water and two cups on a tray. He also arranged Stone's slices with napkins and silverware.

"I'll take the tray," Stone said.

"I'm sure you will, sir."

Stone smirked. "Don't be a smart aleck."

"Don't you blow it," Swenson admonished him while cutting a slice of pie of his own. "I like her. She's special to you. I can see it."

Stone stood there holding the man's gaze. He wanted to argue against Swenson's statement, but his words were stuck in his throat. Instead, he picked up the tray and returned to Addison's room. He could still hear the shower. He placed the tray on a table and went to his room to change out of his damp clothes. When he returned, she was wrapped in one of the guest robes Swenson insisted they stock. She also had a throw pulled up to her chin. She was sitting on the sofa in the sitting room, presumably waiting for him.

Swenson's words came back to him. *She's special to you.*

Stone stood there for a moment, knowing there was no point in fighting what he was feeling. Swenson was right. He'd gone beyond being attracted to her. A switch had flipped inside of him. He wanted her in a deeper, more meaningful way. If he was honest with himself, he'd known that for a long time—way before this visit—which was why he'd let her come to his house when no other woman ever had. This desire for her had been with him; he'd just been calling it sexual attraction and running from it.

Her soft, wanting eyes called to him. "Sit down."

Stone's heart skipped. He sat next to her. He wondered if he'd played himself by inviting her into his life.

Chapter 10

Addison put the last of the key lime pie in her mouth and returned the plate to the tray and picked up her mug for a sip. "I thought I was going to be eaten alive out there."

"Tell me what made you think it was okay to go venturing out—at night?"

"I thought it was close to the house."

Stone shook his head. "We didn't go to east when we left the house. It was the third stop on our tour, so you had no way to know the distance. Bob shouldn't have let you try. I'll have a firm talking to him tomorrow."

Addison put her mug down. "Don't you dare. He begged me to let him take me. I practically raced away."

Stone frowned. "Once you know the layout, it's easy, but I hate to think about how lost you really could have gotten. Running out of gas was a blessing."

"Well, I'm here, drinking tea now, so let it go. If you talk to Bob, I'll never talk to you again."

Stone sat back. He stretched his arms across the back of the sofa and propped a foot on one knee. "Okay. You don't have to come with the permanent threats." She noticed he hesitated before saying his next words. "You're welcome to come back any time. You can get to know the property better."

Addison observed him fidgeting with the hem of his pants. Was Stone nervous for some reason? She couldn't imagine why. Her eyes roamed the full breadth of the room. "I may consider it. The accommodations and guest robes are nice."

"If you steal that, Swenson will most assuredly bill you."

She popped her fingers. "Darn. I was planning to stick it in my luggage."

He smiled, and then his eyes became serious. "You're welcome to anything I have, Addy."

His eyes held hers and she felt like he meant those words from the depth of his heart. Her hands trembled. She reached up and pulled down a piece of her hair and twirled it around her finger. "It's getting late, I think."

"I didn't mean to make you uncomfortable."

"Who said I was uncomfortable? You're the one who's about to unravel the hem of your pants." She picked up her tea again and took the final cold sip.

He slid his hands higher, up to his thighs. "I guess I'm a little nervous because I want to ask you to do something for me."

Addison cocked her head with interest.

"I um…I need a ghostwriter for a book project. I hired a guy, but he's not going to work out. I'm looking for someone else."

Addison returned her mug to the table again. "What kind of book?"

"A story about Black cowboys in Georgia…possibly the southeast. The history and current state."

His words stunned her. "Wow. That's…surprising. Interesting."

"I want to do a few things actually. First would be the adult book and then, maybe a middle grades and elementary version. I'm also going to do a documentary series. I'm planning to put some serious money behind this. It's a passion of mine."

She stood and paced a few steps. "I've never written a book."

"You're a writer. Writers write, right?" He smiled touched his lips; it wasn't toothy, but it was enough to wake the dimple in his cheek.

Her stomach did a flip. *Focus, girl.* She pulled the belt on her robe tighter. She'd already done that three times. She was going to cut herself in half if she pulled it again. Why was she trippin'? The man was trying to hire her. "There are different kinds of writing, Stone."

He put his leg down and edged closer to the end of the sofa. "Do you think you could do it? We could work together on it. My vision, your pen. And you could set it up any way you want."

Disbelieving that, she raised an eyebrow.

"Well, within reason. I mean once the research was all gathered, we could discuss format."

The idea was interesting. Original. With Stone Bennett's name behind it, it would sell. The writing credit would be a gamechanger for her. It could open up the opportunity for other jobs. Ghostwriting paid well. He would pay whatever she billed him. She knew that, but still she said, "I need to give it some thought."

"I can see the gears turning behind your eyes. You're already liking the idea." He stood.

"I don't know. I mean, my boss promised me she would assign me more important work. I've got a few story ideas of my own."

"This is important to me, Addy. I've put it off long enough. I need to get started and I want to work with someone I can trust." He shrugged. "I trust you."

She hesitated before saying, "If I decide to do it, I'd have to fit it in around my other work. You'd have to be agreeable to that."

"Certainly."

"I won't be at your beck and call."

He nodded and then said, "Everyone I employ is at my beck and call, but I'll pay you well for it." The left corner of his lip hitched up.

Addison smiled and shook her head. "You'll be a pain."

He took a step toward her. They were already standing close; he hadn't needed to do that. "I promise not to be. I'd never want to run you away."

She stepped back. "I'll think about it. I really will."

He nodded. "I'll settle for that. Just as long as you make up your mind before you leave." His eyes made quick work of sweeping her body from head to toe, and then back up again.

She pulled her robe together at the neck. "You are pushy."

"There's no doubt about that. If you don't mind, after breakfast, I'd like to show you some of the material I've put together. It might help you with your decision."

She nodded. "I should go to bed. I need to drive tomorrow."

Stone stepped back. He picked up the tray and walked to the door. Before leaving, he turned and said, "Thank you for considering it."

She nodded again and he disappeared, closing the door behind him.

Addison didn't allow herself to think about him. She went into the bathroom, slid out of the robe, and brushed her teeth. She'd been warm for the last few minutes, but with her short nightshirt, she didn't want to let the robe fall open. He'd already been looking at her like she was a whole snack.

And what about the way you've been looking at him?

She dismissed the question and twisted her hair into plaits. When she was done, she climbed into bed and opened her phone. She had a message from her younger sister, Sienna.

Sienna: I'm concerned about Lauren. She missed the christening and Harper's wedding and now she's not going to make it home for Zoe's graduation. What's going on with her?

Lauren's absence was a concern of Addison's as well. Her career as an international photographer took her all over the world, but it wasn't like her to miss big family events. They'd last seen her seven months ago at the opening day for Zeke's soccer team. She'd even been stingy with video chats, claiming Internet issues in the countries she was visiting. Addison knew that was probably true, but still, missing a wedding and a graduation. That wasn't like her.

Addison: I'll see if I can reach her tomorrow and nail her down on why she's not coming.

Zoe, the youngest of the sisters, was graduating from the University of Georgia. She'd finished school in December, but the graduation was being held at the end of May. Lauren knew this, which gave her plenty of time to plan for Zoe's special day. Sienna, a professional event planner, was planning a huge party for Zoe, which included a large guest list.

She closed her message and swiped for her e-reader app. She was about to start reading when curiosity set in. She went to the online bookstore and did a search for Black Cowboy books. She didn't find much at all. Most of the books she did find were for the western part of the country. This was a great opportunity, if for nothing else, to put some money in her savings account. That was always a goal, but did she want to work closely with Stone? Could she continue to spend time with him? Her mind went back to the way he'd looked her up and down tonight. The feel of his strong arms and chest as he carried her from the golf cart to the truck. Not to mention when she shared the horse with him. Those abs.

"He's not asking you to ogle him," she whispered in the quiet of the room. She was doing that on her own.

I'm a professional. The words sounded right in her head, but Stone surprised her. She hadn't expected him to have so many layers. She had a feeling she hadn't even begun to peel them back. And he hadn't really flirted with her since she'd been here. He'd been a complete professional about everything—save for the one offer to shower with him. He just wasn't who she thought he was—which was a complete man-whore. So why did he behave like one when he was in Forest Hills? The man was complex, that was for sure.

***

Addison tossed the comforter off and swung her legs over the side of the bed. It was one in the morning. She still hadn't fallen asleep. The tea. What had she been thinking, not asking for decaf?

She stood, slid on slippers and the robe, and left her room. She needed a glass of water. Once she entered the kitchen, she reached into the refrigerator for a bottle of water, opened it and took a few sips. Instead of going back to her bed, she walked to the Trinity Room, flipped on the light switch, and sat down. The album with the clippings she'd found earlier was on the coffee table in front of her. She put her bottle down and began to look through it.

"Can't wait to get started?"

Her heart lept in her throat at the same time she looked up. Stone was standing there, bare-chested, wearing nothing but men's pajama pants.

Her eyes locked on his chest. Her mouth fell open, and she kept the words that would use God's name in vain in her throat and made them die there.

He walked to the loveseat and joined her on it.

"What are you doing up?" she asked.

"I'm always up."

She frowned. "What do you mean by that?"

"I don't sleep much."

"That's not healthy."

"I'm used to it."

He took over turning the pages for her. Pointing, he said, "This is a picture of my last rodeo team."

Addison leaned forward and took a closer look. They were so close on this short chair. She could smell the warm scent coming off his skin. He must use a cologne, shower gel, and shampoo with the same fragrance. Whatever it was, it was made just for him. The chemistry with his body was unnervingly, delicious smelling.

"You look...so young," she said. *So fine*, she thought.

"I was young," he said, turning his head to look at her. He cleared his throat. "So, tell me, why are you up?"

"I shouldn't have had tea that late. It keeps me up."

"It was decaf."

She frowned again. "Really?"

"Swenson will only serve decaf after 7 p.m. House rule."

She inhaled; his scent hit her nerves and melted her senses again. They both reached for the next page of the book at the same time. Addison felt a surge of heat shoot through her when their hands touched. Stone turned to catch her eyes again. He'd felt it too. He tipped his head toward her. She wanted to move back, but she was frozen there. Waiting for him. Waiting for the kiss she told herself she didn't want.

Stone blinked a few times and raised a hand to wipe across his lips. He turned his attention back to the album. "You are a beautiful woman, Addison." He said the words without looking at her. He said them like he had to get them out of the way so he could move on. He turned the page and pointed at another picture and another like he hadn't just spoken to her inner woman. Addison knew she was what most people considered to be beautiful, but hearing the words come off his tongue in such a genuine and sweet way…disarmed her. Well, he'd already disarmed her, but now he appealed to her.

Black mixed with more Black.

He had her when he said that.

"Any other questions?" he asked.

She glanced at a large, diamond shaped statue on the table in the corner. It reminded her of a question she meant to ask him. "Why Diamond Ranch?"

Stone fell back on the couch and propped his head against his fist. "My mother's name was Diamond."

Addison bit her lip. "How old were you when she died?"

"Almost seven."

"So young."

"Way too young," he said. "She loved horses, so I named this place in honor of her."

Addison nodded. Their eyes connected and held for much longer than they ever should have—again. It was going to keep happening. The chemistry between them was crazy, or maybe she was feeling this way because he was sitting here with his shirt off, looking like Mother Nature made him special.

"I think I'm ready to go back to bed." She wanted to stand, but she was glued to the loveseat.

Stone turned and looked at her. "I have an idea. Something that will help you sleep."

She twisted her neck away from him. "And what would that be?"

"Fresh air," he said, standing. He extended his hand.

Addison hesitated to slide her hand into his. She was already feeling like a victim of her out of control libido; but she did, and then she stood.

Stone led her to the back deck. They stepped out into the cool night air and walked to the edge of it. He let her hand go and she finally breathed.

"Studies have shown that fresh air helps you sleep."

"Really, I never heard that."

"This country air is the antidote for insomnia. I come out all the time," he said. "I have a balcony…off my bedroom."

"I can only imagine what your room looks like if mine is as nice as it is."

"You're welcome to see it." Their eyes locked again. "It's not as nice as yours. I'm pretty simple." He smiled, cockily and added, "Maybe, another time." He turned away from the view, facing her. She was the only thing in his sight as he propped his back and elbows against the railing.

"Maybe never," she said, finally finding her tongue. "I'm feeling sleepy. I think I've had enough air." She turned and walked away from him. Before she could reach the door, he called her name. She did a half-turn in his direction.

"Never say never."

She went into the house. For once, she didn't have a snappy comeback.

Chapter 11

It had been two weeks.

Two long weeks since he'd seen Addison. Why did it seem like an interminable amount of time? Excited wasn't a strong enough description for his feelings. And it had nothing to do with her commitment to writing the book. It was about seeing her. Plain and simple. He missed her. While he found that fact interesting, he also found it scary. He hadn't been excited about a woman since he was twenty-one, and that had gone horribly wrong.

He'd lied to her about never having been in love. He'd been in love all right—with a devil, but he pushed that bit of history out of his head.

The contract for the ghostwriting project was fully executed, so they were in business together. They'd been talking on the phone some, but this week, they were meeting every evening while he was in Forest Hills. The book should have been the thing that got his blood pumping, but it wasn't. It was time at a table or desk or on a couch with Addison. Time looking at her creamy skin, soft curly hair falling in waves around her face. The bend of her neck, the way her eyes twinkled when she discovered something, and then there was the scent of her perfume; it was fruity and floral at the same time. He knew for sure he smelled peaches. She was making him hungry in more ways than one.

He cursed under his breath. What had he started?

His cousins, Zeke and Logan, entered his mind. They were as happy with their new Ingram wives as a horse in hay, but that was luck. Romance didn't work out for everyone. He had the scar on his heart to prove it. He didn't trust his instincts that way. They'd let him down before, left him gutted and alone when he thought he was on a brink of a new beginning. Love was a crap shoot, and he was not a gambling man.

He turned into the parking lot for the studio and pulled his enormous SUV next to Addison's runt of a sedan. Was she frugal or was his old friend, Tom, not paying his writers enough money to drive better cars? It wasn't a bad car, just not nice enough for someone as amazing as Addison. She deserved better. Maybe she would use some of the money he was overpaying her to trade up. Maybe he would buy her one—he could call it a bonus. Who knows, the stubborn woman might just accept it.

Stone removed a garment bag and a small suitcase from his trunk and walked into the building. A greeter ushered him to a dressing room where he was advised he was scheduled for three outfit changes and two location setups...one off site. He inspected the tuxedo and suit that hung on the rack. He put his garment bag next to it and said, "I'll wear what I brought."

The greeter left and returned with the photo stylist, an anxious young woman who looked like she had bad nerves and gas. "Mr. Bennett, I'm Priscilla. I'll be assisting you this afternoon."

Stone took a step back and sat on a stool. "Nice to meet you."

"Sir, we have prepared a wardrobe for you."

"They won't fit. I don't want to stand around with pins sticking in my butt and pricking my ankles."

She blushed. "I assure you; we'll make sure you're comfortable."

"I don't mean to be presumptuous, but you don't have a tuxedo in this building that will fit me better than the one in my bag. It's custom tailored. And I'm only doing two wardrobe changes. I don't want to do three."

Priscilla stood there with her mouth hanging open.

Stone pointed. "You may open my bag to see what you're working with."

Priscilla walked over to the rack and unzipped his bag. She removed a black tuxedo, a navy suit, a pewter gray suit, and jeans and a cowboy shirt. Everything he needed to match was also inside the bag. She cleared her throat. "Well, we were thinking a tan suit for the shot with the horse."

"I'm not trying to look like President Obama on a horse. I'll wear the cowboy outfit. My boots are in the suitcase." He removed his phone and busied himself with a text. When he was done, he noticed she was still standing there looking dumbfounded. "Priscilla, what do you want me to put on first?"

She fought to smile instead of smirking. "The tuxedo, if you would." She walked to the door. "Can we bring you something to drink?"

"I'm good for now."

She left and he changed into the tuxedo. Once he was dressed, he stood in front of the mirror and tugged at his jacket.

There was a knock at the door. "Come in."

In the mirror, he saw Addison peek her head in. His heart thumped. He was too excited to see her. He turned and smiled. "I hate this."

"It was your idea."

"I have so many regrets."

She smiled. She walked up to him and fixed the collar in the back. "You look handsome. I heard you were being extra up in here."

He couldn't help but think she was the one who looked special, and she wasn't even wearing evening wear. Just a white dress with a linen blazer and high-heeled strappy sandals. She was turning him into a foot man. "I only wear my clothes."

"This will be over before you know it."

"It's nice of you to visit with me. I'm a little nervous."

"You've taken a million pictures before."

"But they're about to put makeup on me."

Just then there was another knock on the open door. A woman entered, pushing a cart with makeup items on it. "I'm here to polish your look, Mr. Bennett."

"See," he said. "Ungodly."

Addison laughed. "They're just going to use a pinch."

"I'm already pretty."

Addison laughed. "That you are, but you can always be made prettier. We women endure it all the time."

"That's the price women pay for being God's premium model."

Addison winked. "I'll see you on set." She wagged a finger. "Don't give her a hard time."

She left and the smile dropped from his face, but not his heart. *God's premium model.* He hadn't exaggerated, and God had done good.

Once his makeup was finished, Priscilla returned to his room. "We apologize, Mr. Bennett, the model for your set isn't here. The agency is sending over someone else. She's in route, but she'll be about an hour. Can we order you something to eat or get you a drink?"

Stone groaned. "You've got me sitting here with paint on my face, and you think I'm going to wear it until your model shows up?"

"We can reschedule you if you prefer."

"I don't live in this part of the state, so rescheduling is a no." He pulled the bib from around his neck. He was prepared to leave now, but then he had an idea. "Have Addison Ingram put on the clothes."

"Addison Ingram?"

Stone walked to the door and pointed. "She's the beauty over there by the window. She can do it."

Just then Tom, the owner of the magazine, walked in.

"Mr. Bennett, Ms. Ingram is not a professional model."

"Neither am I, darlin'."

Stone walked out the room and met Tom.

Tom smiled when he saw him approaching. "You know I had to pop over here to see my old friend, posing for my magazine. What have I been asking you to do this for…eight years?"

Stone shook his hand. "At least. Look, your people have a delay. No model for my shoot."

Tom frowned. "What the devil? Let me get to the bottom of it."

Stone hadn't released his hand; he tugged it and said, "No need. I have a plan. We'll ask Addison to pose with me. She's done some modeling."

Tom didn't look sure about it. "You're not going to get me sued for some kind of harassment that hasn't even been invented yet?"

"She likes me. I'll ask her." Stone released his hand and walked to Addison.

"All set?" she asked.

"The model isn't here. I was hoping you'd agree to do it with me."

She laughed. "That's ridiculous."

"You modeled in college, Addy. I remember that."

"For a half hour and that was almost ten years ago."

"You're a prop in the pic. It's about me."

"Don't act like modeling isn't a skill."

"My face is itching. Help me out."

"I don't want to."

"Tom and I…" he nodded in Tom's direction and the man smiled, "… would be extremely grateful. He'll pay you a lot of money for it. I'll make sure of it."

"Some things are not for sale."

"Like what?"

"My dignity."

"What about me?"

"You signed up for this with your little wager. It was bad enough I had to write about it."

"Please, save me from my foolish decision. I'll be grateful. Forever."

Addison put a hand on her hip and cocked her head. "And what does your gratitude get me?"

"I told you. I'll make Tom pay you well."

"You just put a sizeable deposit in my bank account for the book. I don't need the money."

Stone laughed. "If you can't retire, you need it." He groaned. "If you don't care about the money, care about the atmosphere. I'm about to lose my temper."

Addison frowned again.

"I'm trying to refrain from anger and forsake wrath."

She pulled back her head a little. "So, he does read the Bible."

"I never lie."

Now she pursed her lips like she didn't believe him. "I see why you raise horses. That was a lousy sales pitch."

Stone smiled. She was going to do it.

Priscilla approached them. "You are a size six. You can fit the clothes."

Addison rolled her eyes at Stone and walked away with Priscilla. If Addison thought his sales pitch was bad, Priscilla's was worse.

It wasn't long before she appeared, wearing a black knit dress that clung to every curve of her body. It had cut out sections across the left side of the torso and hip. Her hair was pulled back in a tight bun. He loved it; he got to see more of her face. Stone didn't know what the model looked like who was supposed to be on her way, but she couldn't have been more exquisite than Addison was right now.

He walked to her. "You are going to steal the picture."

She blushed, but recovered quickly. "I figured out what I want."

"Please tell me."

"This dress. It's a LaQuan Randall."

Stone laughed. "Do the shoes fit?"

"Yes."

"They're yours." He turned to Priscilla. "Let's get this show on the road."

They were posed, music began to play, and the photographer gave gentle instructions as he took pictures. The photographer was aware neither of them were professional models. He was cautious with them, but it also made the session long because he needed a ton of pictures to make sure he got what he needed for the feature.

"That's good. Stone, get a little closer. Lean in and look into her eyes like she's stealing your heart."

Stone pushed his leg between hers and adjusted the hand on her back to a lower position. "Are you okay?" he asked.

"Uh, huh," she said, pressing her lips together.

He was barely okay. Touching her in this dress was more than he wanted to do this afternoon. Well, he wanted to do it, but not in public. He was struggling to keep his attraction from being embarrassing. He felt like a high school boy.

"Addison, can you relax your mouth? Give him a quaint smile, will you."

She tipped her head back and smiled a little.

"Great. Great. Okay, Stone, put a hand on her cheek; get a little closer to her face. I need you just above her lips like you're going to kiss her."

"No," Addison whispered. She cleared her throat and stepped back. She must have forgotten they were entangled at the legs. She slipped, and he reached for her just as she was about to fall. He pulled her to him, sliding his hands across her back, touching her skin in those open slits of the dress. He stood her upright. "Are you okay?"

"Mm-hmm," she mumbled. "It's hot in here."

"We'll be done in a few minutes," the photographer said. "I just need the almost kiss. Can you get back in the position you were in?"

"If you don't want to do this, I can tell him no."

Addison forehead was dotted with a light sheen of perspiration. "I'm fine."

Stone looked out at the small group watching. Tom smiled slyly at him, like he knew his secret now—that he'd requested Addison for this story so he could have a moment like the one he was getting. The heat of embarrassment warmed Stone's face. He was also embarrassed for Addison. She deserved better than what he'd done to get her to his house. She deserved better than this. She was a professional, not a plaything. He waved to the photographer. "You're going to need to go with what you have." He removed his jacket and tugged at the tie.

Addison placed a hand on his and said, "Stone, I'm fine."

Yes, you are.

"You're hot. You're not a model, and he's taken a thousand pictures. If he doesn't have what he needs by now, he should find a new profession."

Addison smiled like she agreed.

They changed into the second set which was one where Addison wore a white dress, and he wore his cowboy outfit. They drove a few miles to McDonough to a horse farm and took more pictures there.

Back at the building, they went to their separate dressing rooms to change into their clothes. Stone was done first. He stood by the door, waiting to walk out with Addison. Montgomery Robb, one of his high school classmates, entered the building.

"Stone." Montgomery greeted him. "Had I known you were doing this, I would have bowed out, man. I don't like to play second fiddle. Not even in a magazine."

Stone grinned and they shook hands. The truth was, Montgomery Robb's ego was as big as the moon. He didn't think anyone was better looking or smarter than him, but he played the reverse charm game all the time.

Addison came out of the dressing room. Montgomery spotted her at the same time Stone did. She was back in her clothes, her face wiped clean of most of the makeup.

"What's Addison doing here?" Montgomery asked.

"She works for the magazine. She interviewed me."

"I know that, but is she modeling too?"

"My model was a no show. She stepped in for my session."

Montgomery nodded. "Interesting." Stone noticed he never peeled his hungry eyes from Addison as she stopped to chat with the photo stylist and then a few of the other people there. Finally, she approached them. The smile she'd had on her face was replaced with a forced one.

"Addison, so good to see you," Montgomery said. He leaned closer and attempted to kiss her on the cheek.

Addison pulled back, not letting him.

Montgomery was saved from embarrassment by the greeter's interruption. "Mr. Robb, we're ready for you."

Montgomery sighed. "It's showtime." He delayed pulling his attention from Addison, but finally did. "I'll see you on Friday," he said to Stone.

Stone agreed.

Montgomery touched Addison on the forearm. "You look good."

She nodded.

Montgomery walked away.

Addison exhaled and walked through the door. Stone followed.

"Hey, are you okay?"

She was tight lipped. "Of course. Why wouldn't I be?"

"You seem stressed."

"I'm not a model. Pretending was stressful."

Stone was unconvinced.

"What are you meeting with Montgomery about?" she asked.

They walked down the steps. "We're having lunch. Why?"

"No reason really. I didn't know you two were friends."

"We're not. We might be doing some business together."

She shrugged. Not meeting his eyes, she said, "Look, I have a few things to do. I'll see you at six." She walked to her car.

Stone studied her. She was upset about something. Then he realized, she didn't have the dress he'd promised her. Had they said no?

"Wait, your dress?"

Addison was thoughtful for a few seconds, then she shrugged again and opened her car door. "I don't want it anymore." She slid in, started it, and drove away without even saying goodbye.

Addison had a strong personality—stronger sometimes than others, but she was never rude. If he wasn't seeing her for dinner, he'd get in his truck and chase her down for an explanation. Instead, he loaded his things in his back seat. He'd get to the bottom of this later.

Chapter 12

Addison hated Montgomery Robb. Hate might be a strong word. She knew God didn't want her to feel this way, but God didn't have a thing to do with this mess. She'd allowed Montgomery to play with her heart. She hadn't consulted the Lord with a single prayer or notion of one. She'd let a rich, powerful, Godless man sweep her off her stilettos and into his bed over and over and over again for months.

She turned into the subdivision and drove to her new home. It was still a rental, so not hers, but it would be. She had loved it when it was Rachel's and now, she loved that it was going to be hers. She could have chosen to stay in their family house. It was just three miles further down the road and rent free, but the first chance she had to move out, she'd taken it. There were too many memories of their parents there. Too many pictures. Too many knickknacks. Too much everything. None of them could agree on what needed to be packed away and/or donated, so nothing was done. Sienna and Zoe were living in a shrine dedicated to her parents. She needed a space of her own.

Rachel wanted to give the townhouse to her. Her sister was in a position to pay off the mortgage Zeke held on it, but she couldn't take a house from her. She wanted to pay her own way and now she could. With the $100K Stone was paying her, she could make a massive down payment on it and have an affordable mortgage. Okay, maybe she'd be a little house poor, but owning property in Forest Hills had no downside. It was an investment.

Addison entered the house and went straight to the bathroom to run a tub full of water. She needed to wash the day off her body, and a good soak in the tub was the perfect way to get clean and relaxed before she had to meet with Stone. Curiosity had sent her to the photo shoot today. As soon as they asked her to model, she wished she'd stayed in the office, but then once the session began, she'd relaxed and so had he. She'd noticed he was a little nervous, but their natural chemistry made it better for both of them—until that chemistry exploded into sexual tension.

She went into her bedroom and opened the mini-fridge in the corner and removed a bottle of juice, stripped, and climbed into the tub. She told Alexa to play her relaxation playlist and "Runaway" by Aurora came through the speaker. She knew it was the first track. She couldn't deny she'd chosen the playlist for that reason. "Runaway" was the song the photographer played in the background today during their first photo session. Memories of Stone next to her were tapping on her nerves and with this song…she was torturing herself.

Stone Bennett.

Montgomery Robb.

Men like them were the problem with living in a town like Forest Hills. She knew most women would appreciate access to wealthy men like them, but she didn't need them. She could make her own living and her own way. They bought and paid for everything and everyone they wanted, manipulated situations because they could, and none of them were freaking faithful.

Addison closed her eyes against her memory of seeing Montgomery arriving at the baggage claim at the airport with some woman he'd spent the weekend with. He'd just asked her to move in with him. They were serious he said. He was in love he said. She was the right one for him. He'd lied. All lies.

And now there was Stone and all the chemistry that came with him. It was everywhere. He was a player. She knew that. She hadn't even liked him before last week because he'd always been a hound, but something was brewing between them that she was struggling to fight. Maybe the problem was her. She was a magnet for the wrong men, even among the Bennetts. Her sisters were happy with his cousins. She didn't want to be the Ingram who was used and discarded by a Bennett man.

When she agreed to the book deal, she was a bit impressed with him and his project, and yes, she'd felt some attraction between them, but it was small, nothing she couldn't handle, but today...today was different. Her mind went back to the photoshoot.

Stone followed the photographer's prompt. Stepping behind her, he put his hands around her waist. The slits in the dress left space for his hands to touch her skin. Her heart was beating so fast, she thought he might notice the vibrations from her chest. She absorbed the press of him against her back, smelled that sexy cologne he wore, felt the heat of his breath as he whispered in her ear.

Addison tried to force the memory from her mind. He'd told her a joke. Something she couldn't even remember now. He was handling the session with humor, but the intense heat between them...that wasn't funny at all.

She cursed under her breath and closed her eyes again. She hadn't anticipated feeling this attracted to him before she signed the book contract. More memories came to her. This time from the shoot at the farm. She was on a horse, and he was standing next to her, with one hand on her calf.

The photographer said, "Look into her eyes like you're falling in love or trying to get her to fall in love with you." Stone's gaze was serious, his warm, brown eyes mesmerizing. He sucked the air right out of her lungs.

"You look like a queen up there. Beautiful, regal, poised. Pure royalty," Stone said, and then his eyes swept her body. When he returned them to her face, the corner of his mouth hitched into a confident smile. He'd just seduced her right there in a field in front of everyone and he knew it.

The ringing of the phone startled Addison so badly, she jerked up in the water. She reached for a towel and dried her hands before swiping to take the call. It was Stone. She couldn't get away from him.

"Hi, what's up?" She fought to keep tension out of her voice.

"I was hoping you could meet me a half an hour early. 5:30 instead of six. It's the only reservation they have."

She didn't want to meet him a minute earlier. She needed time and distance from him. "We don't have to go to Fontana's."

"Yeah, we do. I like the food." His warm chuckle came through the phone, and she was transported back to the photo session, back to the moment she felt the heated air from his laughter against her neck.

She swallowed and nodded as if he could see her. "Okay, 5:30."

"Addy," he paused. She needed to stop him from calling her that. No one else did. "I was wondering…" He sounded like he had something on his mind. Something serious.

"Wondering what?"

He paused again before saying, "Never mind, I'll see you at 5:30."

They ended the call. She looked at the screen. It was four. She had another twenty minutes in here before she needed to get out and get dressed, so she muted the phone and flipped the spicket for more hot water and pushed thoughts of Stone and Montgomery from her mind. Montgomery was easy, but Stone, he was hanging out on the edges, pushing himself all the way into her head. This was going to be a long week.

***

As predicted, it was a long week. Meeting with Stone every night was a contradiction like none she'd ever had to maneuver through. Being a student of all things Black history, she loved everything he told her about the cowboys. The interviews were enjoyable. She could see the book coming together as she took notes. But sitting with him for hours every night was challenging. Stone's presence across a table was distracting and all-consuming. She had to glance up in his eyes between notes and for questions. They penetrated her whole soul. She had come to enjoy his company. No one could have told her she'd think anything of him prior to her arrival in Mountainville. He had her messed up.

"So," Rachel said, pulling her from her thoughts. "What's it like working with Stone?"

Addison chuckled—nervously. She looked around Rachel's kitchen, noting the small changes her sister had made to the red, black, and white décor Zeke had when he lived in the house alone. She'd softened the edges, removing the black and replacing it with yellow and other small touches that made it more feminine.

She pulled her eyes from the décor and gave Rachel her attention again. "What was that?" Addison asked as if she hadn't heard her. If Rachel knew how immersed she was in her thoughts about him, she'd be praying right now.

"I asked what it was like working with him."

"It's interesting. He knows a lot. He's not just playing cowboy. He's the real thing."

Rachel wrapped her hands around her mug. "The real thing as in a real cowboy?"

"Yes, but also his real love of it. I don't know what I thought about his life up there before I went. I mean I knew he owned a ranch, but—"

"But you weren't thinking about him at all." Rachel raised her mug. "Why would you have been?"

Addison looked down at her own mug. She concentrated on it—way too hard. "Right, why would I have been?"

"Zeke said he was really worried about you when you were lost. He said he'd never heard him sound so scared."

"Well, he was responsible for me. Who wants a dead body on their property?"

"Zeke said he sounds different. He's been different this week."

"Why are you parroting your husband?"

"I'm just making conversation." She shrugged. "And Zeke did say it. I think he's trying to tell me something."

"Like what?"

"That Stone has been changed by you."

Addison laughed. It was one loud, unconvincing guffaw at first, and then she repeated the sound. "That is ridiculous."

"He knows him."

"He's not that close to Stone. He's almost forty."

"Is he?"

"Thirty-seven." She shrugged. "Same thing."

"So what does that have to do with Zeke?"

"They are in two different age groups. Stone didn't even move here until he was fifteen. What was Zeke – nine years old? Then Stone left for Yale. Believe me, they're not that close." Addison pushed her chair back and stood. She took her mug to the sink and turned on the water.

"Leave that," Rachel said. "They've gotten close as adults."

Addison didn't even know why she was arguing that Zeke and Stone weren't close. Maybe she wanted Zeke to be wrong. "Where do you keep the…" She opened the door under the sink and removed the dish liquid.

"Leave it I said."

She turned off the water, dropped her elbows on the counter and placed her head in her hands.

Within seconds, Rachel was behind her, rubbing her back. "Babe, what's wrong?"

Addison stood upright, shook her head. "Nothing. I'm tired. I feel like I'm pulling two shifts, you know."

Rachel was not easily fooled with that excuse, and her words said so. "Don't be afraid of him."

Addison's eyes betrayed her as tears formed.

"You remember what you had to do for me with Zeke?"

"Your situation was different."

"Zeke wasn't much different from Stone. In fact, he was just as big of a player."

"True, but we all knew he loved you. It was a matter of time with you guys."

"Zeke told me Stone is distracted in a different way. Your name comes out of his mouth constantly. He's feeling what you're feeling."

"Yeah, but for how long?" Addison raised a hand to swipe under her eyes. "I can't wait for him to go home. Back to Mountainville."

"Distance doesn't change anything. Remember, Zeke and I had that too."

Addison cleared her throat. She'd had enough of thinking about Stone. "Have you talked to Lauren this week?"

Rachel shrugged. "No. I texted her a few times, but she's been sketchy with her responses."

"Why isn't she coming to Zoe's graduation?"

"I don't know."

"We need to find out. Something is weird with her."

"I agree."

"Look, I'm going to go. I have to get ready for tonight. I still need to get a gift for Lenise."

"I've got one for you," Rachel said, standing. "I even had it gift wrapped."

She left the room and came back with a gift bag.

Addison's shoulders dropped. Relief flooded her. "Thank you. What made you pick something up for me?"

"I knew you were busy. I figured if you had something, I'd keep it for myself."

Addison pointed into the bag. "I know what's in here then."

"You got it." She shimmied her shoulders. "Sexy lingerie, babe."

Addison encircled Rachel into a hug. "Thanks for everything…lunch, the talk."

"I'm praying for you. The same way you prayed for me."

Addison shook her head. "I don't know if it's even that serious."

"Of course it is. You cried. You never cry."

Addison sighed. "I'm good at getting over it."

"Yeah, and I'm sure the kids in Nicaragua would be glad to see you again."

Addison bit her lip. "I'll see you tonight." She raised the bag. "Thanks again."

Rachel walked her to the door. Addison was glad to feel the heat of the sun hit her face when she stepped out. She needed something to make her feel something other than the numb, scared, trapped, confused, wanting emotions she was feeling.

Once she pulled out of the subdivision and got on the main thoroughfare through Forest Hills, her phone rang. She pressed the button on the steering wheel for the Bluetooth.

"Hey, partner."

Her heart made the thump it always did when she heard Stone's voice.

She rolled her eyes. "Hey."

"I know we're not meeting tonight, but I had some thoughts about your question last night."

Addison swallowed. Hard. She was stumped. What did she ask him? She didn't remember.

"I was thinking if you're not busy next month, we could go to the women's invitational in Perry. I could set up some interviews for you…with the women and the organizers. They'll be a great resource. I could pick you up on my way down."

"Yeah, that sounds good." The tone in her voice didn't match her words. "Text me the date."

"Are you okay? You sound distracted or something."

"I'm fine. Just annoyed by the traffic." She came to a stop at a corner and turned on her left signal. There was no traffic.

"Traffic?" he said. "This wouldn't even be traffic in Mountainville."

Addison looked to the left and right and that's when she realized he was sitting in the car next to her. He smiled and waved. Addison shook her head. "I feel like I'm being stalked."

"You know Forest Hills is small."

She did, but still she felt like she couldn't escape him. "This is weird so I'm going to end it."

"Where are you headed?"

"The bank. You?"

"Ethan's. We have some business to discuss and then we're playing cards tonight while you ladies take over Cole's house."

A horn honked behind her. The light was green. "Have fun." She went through the intersection.

"You too," he said. In the rearview mirror, she could see his car turn right. She had a familiar twinge in her chest—like she'd been with him and now she wasn't. Why was she playing hide and seek with her thoughts?

Addison groaned. "That's called missing him." She pushed the button on the dash for the radio and forced herself to think about the words coming out of Leela James' mouth.

She was falling in love with him. Just like she had with Montgomery. It wasn't this fast with Montgomery. Not at all, but still, she was feeling every emotion she didn't want to feel.

She'd prayed after Montgomery. Repented after that relationship and asked the Lord to guard her heart against the wrong man. She'd lost her head with Montgomery, gotten caught up in the romance and gifts. He'd taken her farther than she'd wanted to go. She'd abandoned her principles and all that she'd believed about celibacy, just so she could keep him, and in the end, he'd betrayed her with sex…the thing she thought would keep their relationship together.

She shouldn't have taken the book. The interview was the start of it all, but this week was too much. She'd seen more of him than she needed to see.

"God, please help me not to feel what I'm feeling. I don't want this." She banged on the steering wheel. After a few minutes, she pulled into the parking lot of the bank. She opened the door and sat there listening to Leela sing the story of her life.

Chapter 13

S tone dropped his cards.

Ethan stood and took a bow. "Like taking money from a baby." He raked the poker chips toward him and stacked them.

"You've been lucky tonight. I'll give you that," Cole said, shoving his cards in the center pile.

"I'm horrible at this game. I don't know why I keep trying to play." Rory Bennett tossed his cards in the deck.

"Do pastors play poker?" Stone asked, "Or is this a mortal sin?"

Rory, the founder of a small church on the outskirts of Forest Hills, was used to getting jabs from his family. He'd worked for fifteen years for Bennett International as a vice president, only to quit to walk in what he considered his real calling—starting his ministry. "I'm not Catholic. All the sins are the same and playing a little poker with my cousins ain't one of them."

"Another drink for everyone?" Ethan asked, picking up each man's empty bottle. They all nodded. Ethan disappeared into the kitchen.

"More of those wings," Stone called behind him.

"Where's Zeke?" Rory asked.

"Home with a sick baby," Cole offered.

"So, Lenise has a son already. Do you two have plans to have more children anytime soon?" Rory asked.

Cole hiked his eyebrows. "We are and we aren't. We definitely want children, but Lenise is still pretty young. We have time to just enjoy being married."

Ethan returned with four ginger beers and a platter of spinach dip and chips. "Sorry. No more wings, man."

Stone frowned. "No more wings? What kind of outfit are you running here?"

"One without a cook. Ms. Angie had to fly to New Jersey to help her daughter. She had emergency surgery."

"You should have gotten a temp," Stone said. "Twenty wings for four men is a crime."

"Why don't you just tap the UberEats app and get some more here," Ethan said.

Stone shook his head. "What is that? A city thing? We don't have UberEats in Mountainville. I don't have the app. Plus, it's your house."

"I put some of those hors d'oeuvre things in the oven. They'll be ready in twenty minutes."

"So what's the plan for the bachelor party?" Ethan asked.

Cole shrugged. "We're having it right now."

Stone added, "He won't let me do anything."

Ethan stuck a chip into the dip and popped it in his mouth. "Plan something anyway. Who asked him?" He gave Cole a sideways smile.

"Rory's the pastor, but Cole's being a saint or something. He could at the very least allow me the pleasure of hiring strippers." Stone shook his head.

Cole pointed. "You see, that's why I don't want a party. I don't want strippers."

Stone groaned and twisted the top off his drink. "You don't have to touch them."

Ethan's phone rang. He swiped and turned the phone up and out so everyone could see the screen.

"Zeke!" Stone said. "My man. We miss you."

"He's only missing you because you're a worse poker player than he is," Rory added.

Ethan laughed. "But no one is worse than you, Ror."

"How is the baby?" Cole asked.

"I've got his temperature under control."

"Don't you mean Rachel has it under control?" Stone asked.

"I would mean Rachel if she was here. She's at the bridal shower. I figured no use in both of us missing our night out."

"Which means the nanny is there," Ethan said, and they all laughed.

"Ha, ha, ha," Zeke said. "But yeah, it's true though."

"I can't get him to consent to a bachelor party." Stone took another sip of his drink. "Logan didn't have one. This is getting boring."

"Well, we'll make sure you'll have the biggest party ever, Stone," Ethan said.

Stone took another sip of his drink. "I'd expect nothing less."

The men were all quiet, looking at each other and then Stone. Stone frowned. "What?"

"You didn't say anything like 'I'll never get married,'" Cole replied.

"I'm not getting married. I mean…I don't expect to," Stone said, fumbling over his words.

"Wow!" Zeke said, "He has been roped in for real."

Stone pointed at the screen. "Do you know how corny that is?"

"I think I have to agree with Zeke," Ethan added.

"Somebody fill me in," Rory said.

"He spent the week with Addison," Zeke said. "A few days a couple of weeks ago too."

Stone swallowed. "On business, Ror. Nothing has been personal."

Cole placed his elbows on the table. "Except how you feel about her."

"Let's drop this talk. Who's turn is it to deal?" Stone raked the cards toward himself.

"He's trying to avoid the topic," Zeke said. "He's in trouble."

"Addison and I are in a business contract. That's it."

"And she was just like the only writer you could find in the whole wide world of writers," Ethan interjected.

"Enough," Stone insisted.

"Look, I'm going to eat before the baby wakes up," Zeke said. "You guys have fun. Stone, behave yourself with my sister-in-law."

Cards were dealt for the next round and just before they began to play, the wee voice of Ethan's daughter, Kia, called down from the top of the stairs. "Daddy."

Ethan stood. "Hey, puddin'." He climbed the stairs two at a time until he reached her. He picked her up, and they held a conversation for a minute. Then Kia waved down to the group of them.

"Hi Uncle Cole, Uncle Stone, and Uncle Rory."

They all waved back and spoke in unison, "Hi, Kia."

Ethan took her hand and they disappeared down the hallway.

"I'll check on the food," Rory offered.

"I'll help." Stone pushed his chair back and followed him into the kitchen.

They washed their hands and Rory opened the oven. "Looks done to me." He turned it off, slid on oven mitts, removed the pans, and placed them on the island between them. "So, how is the work for the book coming?"

Stone grabbed a set of tongs from the silverware drawer. "So far, so good. We're still in the interview stage. She's trying to get everything out of my head."

"And working with Addison?"

Stone reached into a pan and started transferring pieces of food to one of the serving trays Ethan had set out.

Rory continued, "I know the guys are coming hard in there."

"Without a reason really." Stone didn't meet Rory's eyes because Rory was good at seeing the truth.

"If you say so," Rory said. "But if you were really interested in Addison for more than a date or two, I think it would be a good thing."

Stone couldn't avoid giving Rory his full attention now. He was about to get some advice, and he needed it.

"It's been a long time, Stone. You need to move on."

"I've moved on."

"I'm not talking about this casual hooking up you've been doing."

Stone swallowed. "You are the only person in this family who knows, and you know because I feel like you're my cleric person."

"Which means I get to give you advice." Rory smiled. "There's nothing to be ashamed of."

"I realize that."

"So, tell Cole and feel free to trust what's happening between you and Addison." Rory put a hand on his shoulder. "You and I aren't kids, Stone. We all want to find our person. God knows, I want to find another woman to spend my life with."

Rory's eyes were sad. The loss of his wife to cancer a few years ago had devastated him. "I'm being a coward, and you don't have a choice."

"Don't compare me to you. We all have our own pain and trauma. What happened to me has nothing to do with what happened to you. What I'm trying to say is grown men do grown men things. Life doesn't have to be this hard, Stone."

Stone exhaled a gut full of anxiety. "I can't deny I like control."

"But cowboys take risks, brother. That's what y'all do."

Stone nodded. He couldn't disagree with that, but a risk with his heart? He didn't know if he'd recover from another bad experience. Could he trust Addison? That was the question he was asking himself over and over.

Rory removed his hand from his shoulder and picked up the oven mitt. "I see your wheels turning. Start by telling your brother. He's your best friend. He should know. And if it becomes appropriate in the future, tell Addison. I have no doubt she can swap stories with you."

Rory picked up a pan and poured the contents out onto a tray. "Man, we don't have all night for you to pick these things up one at a time." He did the same with the other pan. "The food is ready to serve."

"You know that didn't even occur to me," Stone said, picking up the trays.

"See how you made something easy difficult?"

"I got the message, preacher."

"I'm glad I could do a demonstration for you, but I didn't have to use my engineering degree to speed that up. You've got too many servants." Rory laughed and they reentered the room with the rest of the men.

Chapter 14

"It's time to open the gifts!"

Addison sat back in her chair as they all watched Lenise Reid's best friend, Tracy, pull a vintage wooden wagon to the front of the room. All the bridal shower presents were piled high on it and the sign read: **Hitched to Cole's Wagon**.

Such a clever girl, or was it her sister, Sienna's, idea? She'd have to find out.

It was a small shower. Lenise almost didn't want to have one because she had so few friends. The woman was honest about the many years she'd been isolated from other people in her troubled marriage to an abusive, but now deceased husband. The local Bennett cousins—Alex, Karyn, Raven, and Avery— were out in full support of the newest sister to their tribe. With the help of Tracy locating a few old friends and church members, and Sienna's insistence that all the Ingrams be present, she had a nice turnout.

"Please tell me there isn't some silly game where we make a hat or something," Lenise said, cringing.

"We've played enough games for tonight. I'm going to let you open your things in peace," Tracy said, handing her the first gift box.

Mrs. Rose and a server entered the room carrying trays with pieces of cake. Each woman took a slice and settled in to watch Lenise open her gifts. Lenise went through one package after the other, removing mostly lingerie, including the gift Rachel had gotten for Addison. There were some "His and Her" items too. Rachel's gift was a trip to Neiman Marcus to create her own signature perfume. It was the hit of the party. Her conservative, thrifty sister had learned how to spend Zeke's money like a real pro. Addison was proud of her.

"We have one final gift for you," Sienna said, picking up a remote control. "It's from Cole." The lights were dimmed by Tracy and a video began to play on the large screen television.

Cole came on the screen. "Lenise, babe, it's been hard keeping this a secret from you. You know we had pictures from the proposal, but surprise, the video I said was ruined, was not. We have this moment forever. I thought it would be nice for you to share it with your friends tonight."

Lenise squealed with delight. The screen cut to an outside dining setup in front of the Eiffel Tower. White candles and flowers decorated the terrace. Their names, Cole and Lenise, scrolled across the screen. An instrumental version of Stevie Wonder's song "As" began to play.

The scene cut to various shots of Lenise and Cole at locations in Paris. Then there was one where they exited a limo. Cole was wearing a tuxedo and Lenise was wearing a beautiful gold lame dress.

The words "Shangri-La Resort and Hotel, Paris France" popped onto the screen.

The video cut to them entering the outside dining setup. They admired the view and then Steve Wonder was lowered. A violinist began to play. Cole got down on one knee.

Lenise's shock was evident in the video as she asked him, "What are you doing?"

"Loving you forever." He removed a black box from his pocket, tipped it open and presented her with the enormous rock she currently had on her right finger.

Lenise covered her mouth. "I can't believe you. You said this was just dinner."

"Lenise Reid, I love you. I love you today. I'm going to love you tomorrow. I will love you forever. So, if you feel even half of what I feel for you, you will make me the happiest man in the world by becoming my forever."

Lenise's head dropped back. She leaned down to Cole and kissed him before saying, "Yes!"

Stevie Wonder cued back up. Cole stood. He picked her up in the air. They hugged and kissed and opened champagne. The rest of the video was of them during a short photo shoot, dancing, and finally sitting down for dinner together. The Eiffel twinkled yellow in the background. At the end, the words: "The beginning of forever" flashed across the screen.

The lights in the room came back up. Lenise blotted tears. "You all see why I love him."

There wasn't a dry eye in the room. Everyone applauded.

Addison thought it was the most romantic thing she had ever seen in her entire life.

"Go, Cole!" someone hollered out.

"Amazing, right?" Avery whispered. "I didn't know he did all that."

Addison took a deep breath. "I heard a Paris proposal, but that was a lot."

A server filled everyone's champagne glasses.

Lenise continued to blot her eyes to stop the tears. She stood. Her voice cracked with emotion when she said, "I have a special thank you I'd like to make. Second to our amazing trip to Paris, one of the best moments I ever spent with Cole was our first date. I fell in love with him that night. I'm sure of it. We went to a special place, made cookies and just…meeting him, that night came at a time when I really needed it. That date was arranged by Addison." Lenise extended her hands in Addison's direction. "Thank you so much for making that night special for me."

Avery bumped Addison's knee. Addison hunched her shoulders. "It was nothing. I…I'm just glad Cole turned out to be your happily-ever-after."

More toasts were given, and the party came to an end.

Addison raised the glass of champagne she'd been nursing for an hour to her lips and took a final sip. She couldn't wait to leave, so she made her excuses and walked out the door first. Because she and Rachel were the last to arrive, Rachel's SUV was at the end of Cole's long driveway. As she approached it, she could see someone leaning against the front of the vehicle. Stone.

When she got close enough, she asked, "What are you doing here?"

"I'm staying here."

"I know that. I mean waiting out here by Rachel's car."

"I didn't see yours. I figured you rode with Rachel. Being neighbors and all."

"And why are you waiting for me?"

"I missed you." His eyes sank into hers. Like a shy schoolboy, he looked down at his boots and then back up at her. "How was the party?"

"Amazing. Beautiful. Perfect."

Stone grinned. He just stared at her for a moment and then his eyes dropped to his shoes again and then back up to meet hers. "We watched the proposal video."

"So did we."

"I'm rather impressed with my brother."

Addison hitched her thumb over her shoulder. "The women in there would like to clone him."

"He's an original. Always has been."

"How was your men's night?"

"Ethan should be ashamed of himself. I'm starving. Did you have real food?"

Addison shook her head. "We had chick food."

He chuckled and pushed off the SUV. "Let's get something to eat."

Addison hesitated for a moment. She wanted to tell him no, but she couldn't. First of all, she was hungry and secondly, she couldn't deny him if she wanted to. Those chocolate eyes of his weakened her. "Okay."

They got in Stone's truck. She sent Rachel a text.

"What are you in the mood for?" he asked, starting the engine.

"This late? Maybe a BLT from the Hills Diner."

Stone said, "Good choice." He backed out of the driveway.

It was Friday night, so the diner was packed. It wasn't long before they got a table and placed their orders. Stone had the biggest hamburger they served. Addison stuck to her BLT and tomato soup.

He told her stories about his rodeo days. She told him about what it was like to model for the short period of time that she did it. She also told him about her experiences in Nicaragua, and how that was the reason she wanted to write more serious stories.

"It's not that the things people are passionate about don't matter. I think fashion and beauty matter—a great deal. It's just that I've been changed, and once you flip that switch, you can't go back."

He wiped his mouth and took a drink before asking, "What made you choose Nicaragua?"

"Lauren was there. You know her heart is in projects about Black people on the fringes of society, so of course, in Nicaragua, that's the Afro-Nicaraguans. I started Googling about them and before I knew it, I fell down the teaching English rabbit hole. I decided instead of going just to go, I wanted to do something useful."

"You ever want to go back?"

"Maybe," she picked up her glass and took a sip. She decided to not elaborate. Her breakup with Montgomery was the real motivation for the trip, but she'd taken his sour grapes and turned them into wine.

"You should. I'm sure you were great at it."

"The kids need to see more people who look like us." Done eating, she placed her napkin on her plate. "Speaking of people like us giving of ourselves…" she paused. "I forgot to tell you that I found out about your camp."

His brow wrinkled. "You did?"

"I'm a journalist. I know it's not the Harvard Business Review, but I do my homework."

Stone's eyes widened. "Do you think I read the Harvard Business Review? That magazine is for people who are trying to get rich. I'm already there."

She smirked. "I don't pretend to know what you do, Stone."

"You shouldn't discount your work at the magazine. Honest work matters."

"I don't need you to prop me up." She reached into her bag for lip gloss and hand cream. "But why wouldn't you tell me that? You bring a thousand kids from poor areas all over the state to your ranch for the summer. You transport them, feed them, clothe most of them, provide everything and send them home with backpacks full of books and school supplies and gift cards."

He looked annoyed. "Addison, I know what my organization does."

"Why wouldn't you tell me that?"

"Because it's charity, and I don't brag about charity."

"You are there the entire summer, working with the kids daily. That's not just charity. That's a ministry."

"I've got a redeemable quality. Are you really this shocked?"

Addison tilted her head and shrugged. "I don't know. I guess I am..."

His laugh was a rebuff of the insult.

"And it's not that I think you're unredeemable. I don't know that much about you to judge that; it's...I'm blown away. I'm kind of in awe."

Stone focused on his fries, but the tightness of his jaw spoke for him. This was not something he want to talk about, but sharing the story about the camp would make her piece in this trivial bachelor thing mean something.

"Stone, it's inspiring. Inspiring stories give people hope. People want to volunteer. Some want to give money."

Finally, he looked at her. "I don't need volunteers. And I don't need money."

"Inspiration?"

"I prefer to keep what I do for these kids private. They're not charity cases, and I will not have people thinking of them that way."

"What about the coverage on cowboys? That's important to you."

He muttered something that sounded like a curse word before saying, "Do not include it in my story."

She raised a hand, surrendering. "Okay."

Their dessert was delivered. They finished the meal with slices of the diner's renowned apple pie. Once they were back in his truck, he said, "I'd like to show you something."

"Now? It's almost midnight."

"What are you? Sixty years old? It's only almost midnight." He laughed. "It's just ten miles down the road." He reached across the car console and took her hand. "Trust me. You'll enjoy it."

They'd been at odds about the camp story, but holding hands washed the tension away. In fact, the warmth of his touch massaged her entire body all at once. If past excursions taught her anything, it was that when Stone said he wanted to show her something, it was worth it.

Stone put on music. "Going in Circles" by Luther Vandross was up first.

Addison pulled her hand from his and groaned. "You're not seriously going to play Luther Vandross in this car like I'm a date?"

Stone smiled. "I like Luther, and you are a date."

She shook her head. The last thing she wanted to hear was Luther Vandross while she was with Stone Bennett. She took out her phone and scrolled through her social media. She also texted Lauren to call her.

Stone turned off the main road onto a private one that was flanked by trees on both sides. He stopped and cut the engine next to a large, barn-like building. Stone got out and came around to open her door. She stepped out.

"These are the wrong shoes."

"I could carry you."

She'd been in his arms before, and even though she was soaking wet and cold, she still remembered the impact of that. "I'll manage."

They walked to the barn. He pulled the door open. Addison recognized the smell before they stepped in. It was a stable.

"Whose place is this?"

"My cousin. Jackson Bennett. You may not know him. He's a bit of a recluse. He doesn't attend many family gatherings. He and Cole are close. You'll meet him at the wedding."

He walked over to a stall and pet a beautiful, tall, black horse. After a full conversation with the animal, he walked it out of the stall.

This horse was different from the ones she'd seen at the ranch. "What kind?"

"A Percheron. They are a treasure. Strong and smart. They're great for riding. They also compete."

"Are you sure he's not going to be wild? You might have woken him up."

"*Her* name is Minty," Stone said, stroking the animal some more. "She's mine. I trained her and brought her and her baby here. I ride her whenever I come home."

Addison was curious about something, so she asked him. "I notice you always refer to Forest Hills as home. You grew up in Texas and now you've been in North Georgia for years. You didn't even live here that long."

"My family's here, so I guess I think of home as the place where there's people you love." He tossed a saddle onto the horse's back.

Interesting. That's what this man was, and so insightful. He was definitely more than meets the eye.

He removed Addison's shoes and handed them to her. "Don't let her height intimidate you. She's gentle and well cared for." He helped her up and joined her in the saddle. The horse started a slow trot down a trail. They traveled a good distance. At least a few miles. Stone stopped the horse at an elevated observation station. Addison looked out at the Atlanta skyline in the distance. For as far as her eyes could see, the sky was covered in stars and the moon hung low over the city like a ball that could bounce off the buildings at any moment.

Addison was speechless, but she said, "Wow. This is beautiful. I had no idea you could see the city from this far south."

"It's a secret. This is all Jackson's land. He's not trying to let it get out. Then he'll have to run kids off."

Stone climbed down from the horse. He stood there looking up at her. "Can I ask you a question?"

She shrugged. "Sure. I'll decide if I'm going to answer."

He smiled. "What are some things you like, Addison?"

"What do you mean?"

"I mean, I like horses. I like ranch life. I like the mountains. I like leather. I like cowboy boots. I like beer. A big steak. The Bible. Kids. What do you like?"

She was thoughtful for a moment and then she answered instinctively. "I like a good novel. A luxurious hot bath. Designer clothes. Exotic coffee...translation, expensive coffee. Sushi. Music. I like rain and I like to take naps. I don't have one, but I like small dogs."

Stone nodded. "You didn't say writing."

"I thought that was obvious."

"I guess it is," he said, looking out at the view like he was contemplating her words. "Let me get you home. I know it's past your bedtime."

While Stone put the horse back in the barn, Addison walked to his truck and got inside. Stone followed her. He reached for a packet of hand wipes and cleaned his hands and then he opened a bottle of water and offered it to her. She accepted it and took a few sips. Stone opened another one and drank most of it before starting the engine. A welcome flood of cool air filled the car's interior.

Addison put her bottle in the cup holder and twisted her body so she was facing him. "Why did you bring me here tonight?"

"I wanted you to see…" his words trailed off. He tightened his grip on the steering wheel.

"The view?"

He turned and looked at her. "Me."

A little stunned at his answer, she blinked a few times before saying, "I've seen you all week."

"Maybe."

"Sounds like I've been dealing with your representative?"

"No. I don't play games."

"Why don't you own a house here if it's home?"

Stone shrugged. "I never needed one. Maybe that's changing." He pressed his lips together and looked out the driver's side window like the words he wanted to say were out there waiting to get in the truck. He twisted his body so he was facing her too. "I like you, Addison. I like you a lot."

She didn't respond.

"You like me too." He almost smiled. "You didn't think you would."

A slow, lazy smile came to her lips. "No. I didn't."

Stone's response was his own lazy smile. "I care about the book, but I don't care about it more than I care about you right now."

"You should," she said. "You paid me a lot of money for it."

He closed the distance between them a little when he reached for a loose strand of her hair. He pulled it to his lips and kissed it. "Well, I don't." She knew he would kiss her before he did, because she'd called to him with every beat of her heart—for weeks. And it was worth the wait, worth the risk, worth remembering. Addison felt everything she'd been fighting awaken from deep inside her. Her hands found his biceps. He found her neck. She didn't want the kiss to end, but it had to.

Doesn't it?

Yes. Stop!

She pulled back and moved away from him.

He moaned. Actually moaned. "I've been wanting to do that for fifteen years."

Addison didn't reply at first. She just kept staring in his eyes, looking for the truth, wanting to only see sincerity. She wiped her mouth and patted her smooshed hair. "We're working together."

"I've got no regrets. Other than the fifteen years."

She bit her lip. Stone licked his.

Stone reached for the volume knob on the dash. He turned it up and turned it down. He played with it for a few moments. His concentration was high. She could see it in the wrinkles on his forehead. What was he doing? Coming up with his next seduction line? Didn't men like him already have their game together?

Suddenly, he dropped his arm and turned to her again. "You said something tonight, when you described the party."

Not recalling, she waited for him to go on.

"You said it was amazing, beautiful, perfect."

Remembering now, she nodded.

"I was thinking almost the same exact thing about you—just as you were walking to the car. Does she know how beautiful she is? Really? Like how lucky would any man be to be with her? You are amazing, beautiful, and perfect."

Addison pushed back in her seat, away from him. He was good. Thanking him was on the tip of her tongue. It was a compliment, but she was struggling to speak—struggling with this entire conversation because the kiss had stunned her.

Time ticked by—maybe a full minute before Stone spoke again. "I want you."

The beating of her heart intensified. Frowning, she replied, "You can't just have me."

"I'm telling you that I want you."

She couldn't fight rolling her eyes. "What should that mean to me?"

"I don't know, Addy. It's the only thing I can think to say. That, and I'll handle you with care."

She looked straight ahead, out the window, directing her attention at the moon. "You're saying you want to have sex."

"Of course, but that's not all. I mean, I want to spend time with you. I want to get to know you better."

She sighed. "Please take me home."

"Did I say something to make you angry?"

She turned to look directly into his eyes. "No. You did not."

"I'm trying to be honest."

She couldn't resist reminding him of his words. "You told me you're always honest with women."

"I mean, honest about the fact that I feel confused."

She grunted. "You're thirty-seven years old, Stone. You are a lot of things, but confused isn't one of them. You want what you've always joked about wanting from me. I'm not going to be that woman for you. You need to take me home and go find someone else to—"

He threw up a hand. Interrupting her, he said, "I'm not talking about sex. We don't have to…" he paused, "I just told you I wanted it because I do. I like sex. I'm a man. I think about it."

She cocked an eyebrow. "Women don't think about it?"

"Of course you do. I'm not trying to…" he sighed, frustrated. "I'm saying it's your call. Your timing with respect to the next level, but I want to be with you."

"What if I told you it's never going to be before I get married?"

It was him who frowned now. "Why? Are you a virgin?"

Addison was tired of rolling her eyes at this man. "No, I'm not a virgin, but I'm…" she sighed. "I don't want to have this discussion. This is hard."

He laughed. "Tell me about it."

She sliced through him with her eyes. "Don't be crass."

"I'm sorry, but you know I'm crass." He laughed again, more uncomfortably this time. "Give me some grace. I'm out of my element."

"You should get back in it—your element I mean." She pulled her seatbelt around her and snapped it into place. "Please, take me home."

Stone sighed, started the truck, and turned it around to leave. They drove in silence all the way to her house with the sound of the music from his playlist stirring their emotions, or at least hers. When they arrived, Stone walked her to the door. Before she could put the key in the door, he reached for her arm and turned her to him. "If I disrespected you in any way, please forgive me. That wasn't my intent."

"You didn't disrespect me. I'm just not available for what you want."

"I want you. How could you not be available to be yourself?"

"*Myself* doesn't want a relationship. Plus you're a man-whore. Everybody knows that."

"I'm a bachelor, not a man-whore."

"So why so many women over the years?"

"Why not? I'm single."

"Would I be able to do the same? Go out with *all* the men?"

"Why not? It's obvious you're not going to have sex with them. I can't even play Luther Vandross." They were silent for a moment before Stone spoke again. "Addison, I don't want just any woman. I like you. A lot. I want to be with someone I can trust. Someone who doesn't care about my money and someone who can hold a decent, intelligent conversation because I *do* read the *Harvard Business Review*."

Addison tried to keep her face from showing her true feelings. She felt the same. She liked him. A lot.

"Judge me for saying it. Groupies are pretty, but soulless. They're no fun. Not anymore."

Addison knew she should be honest with him. She should tell him why she wasn't ready for what he wanted. She didn't trust him, not only because of his reputation, but because she'd already said she'd never date another wealthy playboy. They took you way too high. The fall was equivalent to dropping from a skyscraper, so instead, she rephrased what she'd said in the car. "I'm working for you. I don't mix business with pleasure."

Stone released a frustrated sigh. He stuck his hands in his pockets. His eyes said he was calculating, thinking, coming up with a solution. She didn't expect him to say, "Okay, we'll cancel the business. I can find another ghostwriter."

"Wow. So, this is how it works with you Bennetts? It didn't occur to you that I might want this job that I've already put a ton of time into, on my resume? That it might lead to other opportunities for me? That I care about my writing career?"

"No. I didn't think of that any more than it didn't occur to you that someone like me would give back to the community without wanting the world to know I was doing it. We all have our biases, don't we?"

Addison was thoughtful. "You're right."

Stone's head bobbed like he was relieved to have made a good point. "Thank you."

"It's late. I'm tired. And weekends are officially for working on your book, so I need to go in and get some rest."

His demeanor changed right before her eyes. "Thanks for hanging out with me tonight." Was that all it took for him—an acknowledgement that he was right? "But think about what I said. We're adults. We can be professional and unprofessional."

His lips slipped into a dangerous smile. She remembered the kiss and pushed her key in the lock. "Good night, Stone."

He walked to his truck, and she shut the door. She'd come close to losing her head. First, there was his passion for his charity. Then the passion that came out of his being, his very pores oozed it. In different ways, both spoke to her heart. If he'd stood there another ten seconds, she was going to kiss him, and God help her if she did that again.

Addison took off her shoes, put her bag down, and removed her earrings. She was headed to the kitchen when three taps on the front door startled her. She went to it and peeked out. *Stone. Why was he back?*

She pulled the door open. He jiggled a hanger with a long, vinyl bag in front of her. "I picked this up for you."

Addison stepped back and let him into the foyer. She took the hanger, hung it over the coat closet and unzipped the bag. It was the black dress she'd told him she'd wanted from the photoshoot. The shoes and jewelry were also included.

"I forgot about—" Before she got her words out, she felt the heat of Stone's body behind her. She turned slowly. He was close. She could feel his heart pumping or was that hers? She wasn't sure.

He tipped her chin up. "I also wanted one more of these." He pressed his lips to hers. She didn't protest, so he became greedy. His lips were on the side of her neck and then they were everywhere again, heating her body, burning away her senses.

He stopped, abruptly. He kissed her on the forehead and stepped back. "I'll leave if you want me to."

Time ticked by—five seconds, ten, twenty. Addison swallowed. She swallowed the word leave. It was followed by good sense and future regret, because she didn't want him to leave. His eyes said he knew. The only thing she could think to say was... "I'm afraid of being hurt again."

Stone stepped closer, taking the space he'd given her. "So am I."

Addison shook her head. "But you have all the power." Tears came to her eyes.

He cupped her face in his hands and pressed his lips against hers again. "No, I don't." His voice was low and husky. "Not when it comes to you."

Addison stepped sideways, away from him.

"I'll do whatever you want. If you tell me to leave, I'll leave, but I don't have the will to go on my own."

She wrestled with the voice in her head that told her to send him away, but the voice in her heart was louder. It wanted him to stay. She raised her eyes to his. "Close the door."

Stone pushed it shut and turned the deadbolt.

Chapter 15

Stone yawned.

"That's the third time. Just tell me if you're bored." Cole reached across the dining room table for a stack of folders and pulled them to him.

"I didn't get much sleep last night."

"That's because you didn't come home."

"Speaking of home. I've been thinking. I should buy a place here."

"Why? Once Lenise and I are married, you can use my guest house."

"I know, but this is my second home. It makes sense."

"Because you intend to be here more."

Stone smiled. "I think so."

Cole whistled. "She must be a special lady."

Stone reached up and scratched his ear. "It's Addison."

Cole nodded. "That was me fishing."

"I like her."

His brother leveled him with a solid look. "You know I love Addison, so be careful with her."

"Don't worry. My intentions are honorable."

Cole let out a humorless chuckle. "You know what they say about good intentions."

"Are you saying you don't trust me?"

His brother's expression didn't offer a bristle of faith.

Stone sighed. "You might be right about me. I've been by myself for so long I…I don't even know how to be in a relationship anymore."

"It's not that hard, man. You just commit to that person. You don't let the other beautiful women spend time in your head. You always show respect. You consider her, more than yourself. You communicate about everything, even the really hard stuff."

"Is that it?"

"Spend money." Cole threw up his hands. "Gifts and surprises are the icing on the cake, but you have to have that baseline of showing up emotionally first."

Stone grunted. "Well, so far, I'm doing all the things you listed. There's no room in my head for anyone else. She's saturated my brain matter. I just thought I wanted to…you know…" He shrugged. "And move on, but I don't want to move on. I want to see her again. I want to talk to her, all the time."

This time when Cole chuckled, he was amused. "This is what you call falling in love."

"I've been in love before. It wasn't nice."

"That's because it was probably toxic."

"Maybe. Maybe it was me."

"Do you want to talk about this mysterious relationship I don't know anything about?"

Rory's words came back to him. *Tell your brother.*

"I uh," he hesitated. "I'm about to shock you."

Cole encouraged him with a nod.

"You remember the mess with my first foundation?"

Cole squinted. "Cowkids. How could I forget?"

"Yeah, I never really told you everything that happened with that." Even to his own ears, his voice was woefully sad. Thinking about what he was about to tell his brother caused regret to explode in his gut. He released a long sigh before sharing his long overdue truth. "The president of my board was a woman named Nancy Francis."

Cole leaned forward. He put his elbows on the table and made a tent with his fingers in front of his mouth. "Go on."

"She was my wife." Stone watched his brother's eyes grow big and then bigger and then confusion clouded his face. He continued, "That's why I hung around in Connecticut after graduation."

"I asked you about that."

"She was pregnant. And though we always used protection, I believed it was my baby. You know mishaps happen. Birth control fails." Stone shrugged. "The truth is, I was in love. I believed everything she said. We went to the courthouse right before the baby was due. I was about to bring her home to Forest Hills so you all could meet her and then…"

"Then what?"

"She admitted she lied. It wasn't my baby. She'd been seeing her ex when she got pregnant. She was still seeing her ex the entire pregnancy and after we got married. She wanted out of the marriage so she could go be with him."

Cole's forehead was wrinkled like a walnut. Stone knew he wouldn't see judgment in his brother's eyes, but he waited for disappointment before he finished his story. It didn't come. Rory had been right, and it felt good to get this off his chest.

"The charity was something I wanted to do, but she pushed me to start it. She said all she ever wanted to do was help the poor kids in Bridgeport. We had like visions and passions. I bought it. Every word. But it was a setup from the beginning. Everything was in both our names." Stone tossed his hands up. "You couldn't have told me that I didn't know everything about her, that I wasn't building something with someone."

Cole sat back. "Man, this is a lot."

"I know."

"A whole wife."

"She wasn't whole."

"I'm glad you said it." A beat of silence passed between them before Cole said, "All women aren't Nancy."

"But the thing is…I don't trust myself like that. Not anymore. I mean, I didn't see a single sign that she was duplicitous."

"That was fifteen years ago. You were young."

"Feels like yesterday."

"But it's not." Cole shook his head for emphasis. "How come you never told me about this?"

"Embarrassed. I'm the older brother. I'm supposed to lead by example. That's what dad always drilled into me." Stone rubbed his hands up and down his pants leg. "But Rory reminded me of something last night. You are my best friend. You're not just my younger brother. Not anymore. You haven't been *just* that for a long time."

Cole reached across the table and offered Stone his fist for some dap. They both smiled and pounded. Cole smirked. "So, Rory knew before me?"

Stone shook his head. "It was a confession kind of thing, man."

A door opened in the hallway and heels clicked on the wood before Lenise blew into the room. She was carrying a shopping bag. Stone recognized it was from their friend, Robin Pendleton's bakery, Sweet Delights. Lenise kissed Cole and offered Stone a greeting. "Good morning, Future Brother-in-Law." She slid out of her jacket and sat on Cole's lap. "Look, I know you two are working, but this is urgent wedding business. I need ninety seconds."

Cole took her hand and said, "Babe, we were in the middle of something really important."

Stone stood. "I was done. You two can talk."

"No, sit," she said, pointing at Stone's chair. "I want your opinion too."

Lenise reached into the bag and took out four cakes boxes and two spoons. She slid two boxes in front of Stone. "Robin is having trouble getting Queen Strawberries."

Cole lifted a brow. "The ones from the Tokyo? Can they use king berries from down the street?"

Lenise smirked. "You're real funny. This is serious business. I have to change the cake filling. Tell me which one you like best." She opened the box in front of her and Cole and stuck a fork in one piece and put it in Cole's mouth.

Stone opened his and took a bite. Then he ate some more. "I like this."

"Me too," Cole said.

"Okay," she said, looking pleased with their progress. "Drink some water. It'll clear your palate."

They both had bottles, so they did as she instructed.

"Now try the second one."

"Baby, I like the first one."

She gave Cole a look that let him know he was trying both cakes. Stone laughed and opened the second box.

Cole stuck his fork in and tasted. After a few seconds, he said, "This is great."

Stone put his two cents in too. "I agree. You can't go wrong with either one."

Lenise stood and planted a hand on her hip. "I need you to help me choose."

"Babe, I have a great idea. Go get Jax. Whichever one makes him squeal the loudest is the cake for us."

She pursed her lips. "You're not helping me."

"I'm just trying to include the whole family." He pulled her to him and kissed her hand. "I like the lemony one."

Lenise smiled. "Me too." She looked to Stone, awaiting his opinion.

"Me three."

She clapped. "Great. It's decided. I'll let you get on with your business. I have to run back out. Stone, will we see you for dinner?"

"No. I'm headed home this afternoon."

She walked around the table. He stood, and she gave him a hug. "Drive safe."

Then she left the room.

Stone sat. "She's as sweet as she can be."

"She's amazing, you know. Just perfect."

Stone remembered his thoughts about Addison last night.

Amazing.

Beautiful.

Perfect.

Cole picked up the cake plate and finished the remaining bit of the small piece. "I was in love on our first date. I felt like I could look into her eyes for the rest of my life. It was just a feeling, you know?"

"And then you had trouble?"

"All couples have trouble. It's not a reason to give up on your relationship," Cole replied. "That is unless like I said before...it's toxic."

There was that word again. Rory had also mentioned toxicity.

"Clearly, Nancy was the extreme version of toxic, but what would you call a normal level of toxic in a relationship?" Stone asked.

Cole's frown was concerning. "Man, there's no normal level of toxic."

"I don't know anything but what Nancy put me through," Stone said. "I don't even know what to expect in a relationship."

Cole shrugged. "Toxic is whatever makes your skin crawl, man. No one is happy unless it's them and they're typically happy because they have drama. Abuse, lying, cheating, and stealing are toxic, but differences of opinion…issues that need deep conversation and compromise—that's normal. That's navigating your human stuff."

Stone rubbed his jaw and pushed further back in his chair. He didn't have the energy for this conversation. Plus thoughts of Nancy had him rattled and unsure of himself. He hated that. He pointed at the pile of work. "Let's finish this paperwork. I need to take a nap and get on the road."

Cole picked up the first folder and slid it across the table so that it landed in front of Stone. "I'm glad you told me, but it took you long enough."

Embarrassed, Stone dropped his eyes to the file folder. "I think I was planning to take it to the grave."

"Let me know if you want to talk some more. I'm here for you." Cole raised an index finger. "I've got to say this last thing though." He paused, and Stone knew it was going to be a gut punch. "You and I have handled ourselves differently with respect to women. I think you having *all* you want has made it easy for you to pass on a permanent commitment."

As predicted, Stone felt his brother's words in his gut.

"I'm not judging your choices, but it's like you said, I'm your best friend. I'd love to see you with your special somebody." Cole picked another folder off the pile and opened it. "It's a beautiful thing."

Stone was humbled by his brother's care. He also knew he was right. It had been so long since he'd been a one-woman man that he'd forgotten what it felt like to care for one woman. Addison was changing that. "I'll take all under consideration."

They got to work. Stone tried to put his attention on the documents in front of him, but his mind was back at that townhouse where he'd spent the night. He was still with Addison.

Chapter 16

Addison threw the comforter off her body and pushed herself out of the bed. She'd fallen back to sleep after Stone left this morning. She picked up her phone. She had a text from Rachel.

Rachel: There was a really big truck in your driveway this morning.

Two surprised face emojis followed Rachel's words.

Addison: Mind your business.

Rachel: I want details.

Addison shook her head and replied: The details aren't exciting.

Rachel: Shocked emoji.

Rachel: Don't tell me you sinned and didn't even have a good time!

Addison laughed and went to the bathroom. She showered and made coffee. Just as she was about to sit down in front of her computer, the doorbell rang. She answered. A delivery man was standing there with the biggest bouquet of roses she'd ever seen.

"Addison Ingram?"

"Yes."

"These are for you." He slid them into her hands and picked up a box she hadn't even noticed on the ground next to him. "These are vases, ma'am. Just in case you need them." He put it inside the door and walked away.

She pushed the door closed and took the flowers into the kitchen. There had to be four or five dozen of them. He must have gotten every rose they had in Forest Hills. She placed the bouquet down and pulled the card from the holder.

Because you like them.

~ Stone

She smiled. Her phone pinged again.

Rachel: Somebody thought last night was exciting.
Addison: You are turning into a crazy neighbor.
Rachel: You know the nursery faces the front.

Addison shook her head. She went to the door for the vases and split the bouquet up into four arrangements. Then she called Stone.

She could hear wind in the background. He was on the highway already, and she was missing him already.

"I'm guessing my delivery arrived."

"They are ridiculously beautiful."

"Just like you."

"Thank you."

"It was my pleasure. I enjoyed the time we spent together last night."

"So did I." Addison cleared her throat. "So, where are you?"

"North of Marietta."

"Did you sleep in?"

"I had an early meeting with Cole for Bennett Giving. You know he's always asking for money."

"You should have waited until tomorrow to leave."

"I need to get home. I have important business on Monday."

"I'm going to do some writing."

"Good. You're on a tight deadline," he said. "Look, darlin', I'm getting a call from the ranch."

"Yeah, go."

"I'll call you tonight," he offered.

She stiffened. Perspiration popped out on her forehead like she'd walked into a sauna. Now she would be expecting him. What if he didn't call?

"Addy, tonight, okay?"

Was he already reading her mind? "Okay."

The background noise was gone and then so was he.

Addison opened the files for the book and started sorting through it all. Her phone rang and she saw Lauren's face appear for a video chat.

"Hey, I've been trying to reach you."

"I know. How's everything?"

"Zoe is heartbroken."

"She doesn't have to be. I'm coming to the graduation, but don't tell her. I want it to be a surprise."

Addison clapped gleefully. "Great!"

"But I can't stay. I have to fly right back out."

"What do you mean you have to fly right back out?"

"I'll meet you all at the graduation and then the party for a little while. I have to catch a flight at seven p.m."

"Lauren, a same day turnaround?"

"It can't be helped."

Addison was disappointed and she didn't hide it. "I guess we have to take what we can get."

"You'll have all you can stand of me soon enough. I'll be coming off the road at some point this year. I'm trying to make as much money as I can while it's good."

"You sound stressed."

"I'm not, but I need to go."

Addison tried to resist protesting, but she wanted to talk about Stone. Harper and Rachel were in Bennett man heaven. Neither was good for older-sister counsel right now. "Wait," she cried, "I have things to tell you."

Lauren huffed. "Is anyone sick?"

"No."

"Then text me or tell me when I see you. I love you." Lauren blew a kiss and ended the call.

Addison couldn't shake the feeling that something was going on with her sister. Lauren was acting weird. She planned to get to the bottom of it when she arrived next week. But for now, she focused on her work. She spent a few hours reading through the interviews she'd had transcribed from her conversations with Stone. When she'd done all she could do, she stood and stretched. There was a knock at her door. She peeked out. Harper, Rachel, and Sienna were standing there. She pulled the door open.

"So, we hear you had a big truck in your driveway all night," Harper said. "We are here for the details and possibly a prayer session or exorcism. We can even make a Stone Bennett doll and stick pins in it. Whatever may be required."

Sienna raised a few boxes of pizza. "And we brought dinner."

Addison rolled her eyes and laughed. "Come in, you bunch of voodoo priestesses."

They made their way past her. Addison shook her head and closed the door.

Chapter 17

Watching their baby sister walk across the stage to accept her college diploma was an emotional moment for all of the Ingram sisters. It also represented the culmination of the promise Lauren made to their dying grandmother—to make sure everyone got an education. Zoe was the last of them. The burden of being the stand-in parent was lifted for Lauren. It was obvious in the heavy sobbing she'd done the entire time. Addison had never seen her cry so much. She couldn't help feeling like there was more to it, especially since Lauren had been so evasive this year.

After exiting a limo, the six of them walked into the ballroom of the Bennett Atlanta Hotel. Friends, family, church members, and neighbors were waiting to celebrate Zoe. Sienna had planned a delicious party—everything from the decorations to the food was the best. She'd outdone herself for Zoe.

"I can't believe we're all done with school," Lauren said, picking up a glass of water and taking a long drink.

Addison's eyes dropped to her sister's glass. She hadn't had one glass of wine and had only drank a half a flute of champagne. Not like her. She also looked exhausted, nearly drawn, which was also not like her. Her hair was thin. Travel was hard on some, but it seemed to invigorate Lauren most of the time. Not today. Was she sick? Something was off.

"So, you said you have to head back out," Addison said, confirming what Lauren had already told them. "Why such a rush?"

"I made the commitment months ago."

"You knew when Zoe was graduating a year ago," Sienna said.

Lauren sighed. "This is a once in a lifetime project. I didn't want to pass on it."

"Not even for us?"

Lauren put a napkin down and started folding it. She made eye contact with no one. "I'm here, aren't I?"

"But we haven't seen you in almost a year."

"I promise it won't be long before I'm home for a visit. I told Addison I'm planning to take a break. I may be home for a considerable stretch."

Sienna snatched her head back. "What's considerable?"

"A year off."

"What?" Sienna almost spilled her drink.

Addison's concern heightened. A year off. Again, illness came to mind. "I can't imagine you in Forest Hills for a year."

Sienna raised her champagne flute and sipped more. "And so extreme, from no visit to a long visit."

"I am a freelancer. I get paid when I work, so I have worked hard so I can take a break. I miss you all." She flicked her wristwatch around to look at the time. "Where is Harper? We need to get this family picture out of the way."

Sienna shrugged. "With Logan I guess."

"Probably in his office on the desk. Those two can't keep their hands off each other," Addison said.

Lauren tossed her hands up. "Well, it was a long time coming."

Sienna pointed. "Look, there she is."

Addison and Lauren looked in the direction of the entrance. Logan and Harper entered with Ethan.

The momentary joy that had been on Lauren's face disappeared behind a frown. "Why is Ethan here?"

"I invited all the Bennetts. I figured Zoe would get her student loans paid off tonight." Sienna giggled.

Lauren rolled her eyes. "Speaking of Bennetts. How is the work coming with Stone's book?"

"Slow, but good. It's a big job, and I've never written a book before, so I'm learning as I build the plane."

"And using cliches I see," Sienna teased.

"Interesting he hired you for it," Lauren interjected. "I mean, I know you're simply amazing and capable of anything, but speaking as a photographer, there are some things I wouldn't be good at photographing. All writing isn't the same either."

Addison could see Lauren was fishing, or rather setting her up for the next question, which was sure to be about her relationship with Stone. Sometimes her sister was direct, other times, she angled for an opening. She was angling.

"What I lack in experience, I make up for in enthusiasm."

Lauren twisted her lips. "Uh, huh. I heard he stayed over."

Addison played with the stem of her champagne flute. "Rachel talks too much."

"You're not one for casual sex. Is there something we need to talk about to make sure you're okay?"

"I could ask you the same thing," Addison responded. "Actually, I am."

Lauren squinted and looked over Addison's shoulder. Addison turned to find Harper, Logan, and Ethan approaching. They took the empty seats vacated by Rachel and Zeke, who were on the dance floor, and Zoe, who was taking pictures and talking with her friends.

Ethan went right for Lauren. Addison watched as he practically devoured her with his eyes. "It's good to see you, Lauren."

Lauren simply said, "Likewise." Her curt tone told the real truth. She was anything but glad to see Ethan.

If he noticed, no one could tell. He kept right on lapping up to her like an attention starved puppy. "You look good."

"I have jetlag, and bags under my eyes, but thank you for the generous compliment."

Ethan chuckled. "Fishing for another one—like, 'I can't tell you're jetlagged.' Or maybe, 'You look beautiful as always.' He tapped her wrist with his index finger. "If I said it, it would be true."

Touching her seemed dangerous, but then their eyes connected, and they melted into each other for a moment. Pulling her arm away, Lauren broke the stare. She turned to Sienna. "Can we take the family picture now?"

Sienna was game to rescue her big sister. She stood, saying, "I'm going to gather Rachel and Zoe. We're going to take the photo at the picture wall. Freshen up the lipstick, powder your noses, and come on." She left and went to interrupt Rachel and Zeke.

Addison watched the dynamics play out between Lauren and Ethan as they sat there with him gawking and Lauren trying not to pay attention to him when it was obvious they were magnets that couldn't be pulled apart. Addison freshened her lipstick as she'd been told and powdered her nose. They joined the other three sisters on the picture wall and took a series of shots before Lauren hugged and kissed them all. Addison followed her out the door.

"I'm concerned about you," Addison admitted.

Lauren sighed. "Why?"

"You don't seem yourself. And now you're talking about a year off. You aren't sick are you? I mean, you'd tell us."

Lauren smiled. "Honey, I'm fine. I'm just...I need to come off the road for a while and figure out what I want to do with my life."

"I thought you were happy with your life."

"I am, mostly, but I..."

"Want a family," Addison interjected. She understood.

Lauren shrugged. "To start, I just want a personal life. Even an extrovert like me gets tired of living her life with strangers."

"I hate to ask the obvious."

"So don't. I'm not interested in Ethan." Lauren reached around her neck and hugged. "Speaking of men who can't be trusted, be careful with Stone. He's the worst of the litter and you know it."

"It's just business."

Lauren sighed. "No, it's not." A taxi pulled up and stopped. "This is my ride." Lauren squeezed her hand. "Go back in. I'll let you know when I get to the airport."

Addison nodded and watched her sister's ride disappear. She went back into the party. The only person sitting at the table was Ethan. Everyone was dancing. Addison wasn't in the mood, so she rejoined Ethan at the table.

"I don't see Lauren," he said, looking around.

"She left."

Ethan looked like all the joy left his soul. "She's not coming back?"

Addison hated to be the one to give him the bad news, but she was stuck with the job. "She's headed to the airport. She has a flight out in a few hours."

Ethan yanked at his tie like it was the reason for his disappointment. "I didn't know she was in town."

"She just came in today."

Addison watched his Adam's apple go up and down sharply. Regret was a big pill. "In for the graduation and out the same day?"

"That's the life, I guess." Changing the topic was a must, and she knew he was always ready to talk about his daughter. "How are you? How's Kia?"

"Kia's great." He raised a hand and rubbed his chin. Addison noticed he hadn't answered about himself, but she didn't push. He was sad and lonely…just like her sister. She couldn't help wondering if they'd be happy together.

"I haven't seen her in a while."

"You are welcome to come for a visit and take her off my hands anytime."

Addison laughed. "I might just do that."

"It would be nice, considering her mother has disappeared." Ethan shook his head. "Completely."

Addison mused. Money certainly didn't solve all problems. "I'm sorry to hear that." She took another sip from her glass, watched the people dance and mingle about until she couldn't fight asking her question anymore. "Ethan, I don't mean to pry."

"It's not me," he replied, like he knew she was going to ask about the rift between him and Lauren. "It's your sister."

"I was too busy being a teenager when you were dating her to notice how serious or not serious your relationship was." Addison paused. "I said I didn't mean to pry, didn't I?"

He drummed his fingers on the table. "Just…pray for her heart. I broke it, not intentionally, but I did, and I can't get her to forgive me. I want her to, so badly."

Addison nodded. Montgomery flashed through her mind. Her chest tightened. She wondered if she'd forgiven him. He hadn't asked, not like Ethan. Did unforgiveness keep you connected to exes? She wondered.

Ethan's question broke through her thoughts. "Is Stone on his best behavior?"

"He's been a complete gentleman."

Ethan smiled. "He's a good guy. He's got a good heart."

Addison cleared her throat. "I think I've had some surprises."

Ethan's smile deepened. "Hopefully, he won't blow it."

She raised her glass again, hiding her expression. "Blow what?"

"Anything or anyone that might be good for him." Ethan stood. He removed an envelope from his jacket and placed it in front of her. "I'm going to go. Give this to Zoe for me."

"Of course."

Addison watched him walk away from the table and out the door. She felt bad for him. She also felt bad for Lauren. She didn't know what happened between them, no more than what Harper and Rachel speculated. He dumped Lauren for Lucy and married her, but it was obvious he'd made a mistake. The marriage hadn't lasted more than a few years. But she wasn't going to judge what her sister should or shouldn't do. There was nothing Montgomery Robb could say to make her take him back. But then did she ever really love Montgomery, or was she in merely in love with the idea of being in love? She'd fought answering that question for years, because if it was no, it meant she'd never been in love. What did that mean for someone her age—to never have loved?

The celebration ended with more champagne and cake. Zoe was on to the next party with her friends, so once it was over, they went back to Rachel's house.

"Did anyone get the story on Lauren's in and out visit?" Rachel asked, opening a bottle of some fancy juice and pouring four glasses.

Each woman reached for hers. Addison took a sip. "I think she's burned out. It sounds like she's coming home."

Rachel sat and pulled her legs under her on the couch. "We'll see, won't we?"

"How is the work on the book?" Sienna asked.

"Slow. I try to work for two hours a night when I get home, but there's so much research."

"Maybe you should take a leave of absence from the job," Harper suggested, stretching out on the sofa.

"No. I've just gotten an assignment about the school system in Fulton. This is the break I've been waiting for. It's not time to quit." Addison tapped the sides of her glass and then took a sip. "I'll manage."

Her phone pinged a text. She looked down at it.

Stone: You wanted to interview a cowgirl. I have one.

She typed out the text: You probably have a lot.

Her finger hovered over the send icon. He was talking about business, and she was flirting. She deleted it and put the phone down.

"Is there something you have to do?" Rachel asked.

"What makes you think that?"

"The smile on your face as you typed."

Addison shook her head. "It was a funny message."

"From whom at this time of night?"

"You act like it's midnight. It's nine p.m."

Rachel took another sip of her juice. "That was a big smile."

"Where's my nephew?" Addison asked, looking toward the stairs.

"Sleeping like the good baby he is," Rachel said. "Don't try to change the subject by deflecting."

"There's nothing to deflect." She clasped her hands and twisted her energy into them. "It was from Stone. The text *is* actually about the book."

"So why the big smile?"

"Because." Addison stood. She finished her glass and picked up her purse. "He makes me smile." She threw up her hands. "There. I said it. I like Stone

Bennett. A lot. I know it doesn't make sense, but I do."

"Where are you going?" Harper asked, sitting up.

"Home. I'm tired. I have to drive downtown for a meeting in the morning."

Addison hugged each of her sisters and then left. Walking across the cul-de-sac to her townhouse was convenient, but Rachel shared they would be house-hunting soon. Even though they were buying a house near the soccer stadium Zeke owned with his business partners in Charlotte, they also wanted a larger house in Forest Hills. Zeke needed to entertain soccer people.

Addison entered her house, kicked off her shoes, and collapsed on the loveseat. She looked around the room. She could still feel the masculine energy Stone left behind. She shouldn't have let him in that night.

She texted him back: **Good. I look forward to talking to her.**

The ping with his response was nearly instant.
Stone: Do you have time to talk?

She sighed. "About what, Stone?" She didn't respond. Instead, she video called him.

"There she is," he said. He was out on the deck. She recognized it. The moon was full and glowing like it was its mission to brighten Stone's face in the camera. He looked good. "How was the party?"

"It was really nice. Crowded."

"Good for Zoe."

"She got a lot of nice gifts."

"I sent her one."

He was full of surprises. "Did you?"

"Yep."

"Thanks. She's out partying with her friends now." Addison stood and walked to the back door. She opened it and stepped onto her own deck where she realized Stone hadn't stolen the moon completely, but it was nothing like his view. "To be young and right out of college. Those were the best days."

The smile Stone had slipped from his face for a moment. He looked over his shoulder at the moon, and then turned his attention back to her.

"What was that?" she asked.

"What was what?"

"I said to be young and right out of college and you looked like someone kicked your horse."

"Nothing. It was so long ago I don't remember."

"So who's this cowgirl?" Addison asked, moving to the railing and leaning over it.

"She won a regional rodeo last year. She's from Augusta, so not too far. She's coming to a competition next month."

"Okay." Addison moved the phone from one hand to the other and planted her chin on her fist. Quiet fell between them.

"I kind of miss you, Addy."

"Miss me?"

"I'm used to talking to you every day."

"Is that why you texted me about an interview that's a month from now?"

He smiled. "I guess it is."

"Well, I guess if you can share your truth, I can share mine."

Stone's smile widened enough for his dimple to appear.

"I haven't missed you at all."

He laughed and threw his head back. "Why so cruel, Addison?"

She smiled at her own teasing. "That's what you get for having all of the moon there."

"It's always like this. Mountains are high elevation. We see it more." They were both silent again before he said, "You should come up."

"Come up for what?"

"A visit."

"Well," she dragged it out. "I *am* pitching my editor on a story I want to do about Black cowboys."

"Really?"

"Yes. If she says yes, I get to double dip. I can get paid for this book research twice."

Stone laughed. "Am I not paying you enough?"

"It's an interesting story. Who knows, I may make it all about the cowgirls."

"Funny you should say that. I had a conversation with Tom about it the other day. I kind of mentioned the same to him. It was in passing, but he seemed interested, so it should be an easy sell."

"I don't talk to Tom."

"Well, tell your editor you have it on good authority that Tom would like the idea."

"She has a few bosses between her and the owner." Addison shifted her weight from one foot to the other, just like she was about to shift the conversation. "I didn't know you talked to Tom on a regular basis."

"We share a mutual business interest, so I do. Anyway, he thought it was interesting, so you better shoot your shot before he pushes it down, and it gets assigned to someone else. I didn't mention your name. I figured you'd get all funny about me doing that."

"I would," she said, leaning into the camera for emphasis. "The Atlanta bachelors article is coming out in ten days."

"That right? That's fast."

"The e-version. The actual paper magazine releases on the first of July. I'll send you the proof when I get it."

"No need. I trust you."

"You need to be prepared for all the women who will be after you."

"I'm ready to fight 'em off."

"All of them?"

Stone licked his lips. "You've already got my attention. I think you know that."

God, he made her feel like a schoolgirl with a crush. He was so direct. She wasn't used to it. "I guess I'll see you in what, two weeks?"

He frowned like he didn't remember.

"Your brother's wedding."

"Yeah, plan to save a dance or two or all of them for me."

"I will do that," she said.

"Good." He nodded. "I'll let you go. I know you have to work tomorrow."

"So do you."

"Yeah, but we know I don't sleep."

"You slept the night we were together." She held her breath. She shouldn't have brought that up.

"That I did." His lips slipped into a smile. "Maybe I just need the right person next to me."

Addison's breathing stopped. Did this man ever say the wrong thing? Not lately.

He licked his lips again. "You rest well for both of us. Good night, Addy."

Addison swooned. She loved when he called her Addy. "Good night." She ended the call.

She looked up at the sky. The moon had come out from behind the clouds and filled the small space the stars left for it. She wondered if Stone was still standing on his deck looking at it too. She started to wish on a star, but it wasn't her way. She didn't believe the stars lined up to make things happen. She believed good and perfect gifts came from God.

"If he's for me, let it be, but God, if he's not, please show me. Show me before I fall in love."

She'd never prayed before getting involved with a man before. She learned the hard way that was a mistake. She looked back at the sky, past the moon and yearned for heaven to protect her heart.

Chapter 18

B eth was more than happy to let Addison do a feature on Black Cowboys of Georgia. She also liked the idea of including cowgirls as a separate story within the story.

She'd only been joking about being paid for the work twice, but this would free up some time for her. She had all the research already, so writing the articles would be a breeze. She just needed pictures and she could get quite a few of them when she went to some events with Stone. She also had an excuse to go to Mountainville.

Addison was still smiling about the story approval when she arrived home to find a beautifully wrapped box on the island of the kitchen. It had to be a gift from Rachel. She had a key. She opened it and was thrilled to see it was coffee. It included packages of Jamaican Blue Mountain, Costa Rican Original, Brazilian Estate Coffee, Ethiopian coffee, and something from Japan that was labeled in Japanese. The card was signed:

For the woman who likes expensive coffee.

Enjoy!

Stone

She pulled the card to her lips. This was so sweet. Once she was settled, she called him.

"My first delivery was received."

"First?" she asked curiously.

"It's going to be a good week for you, darlin'."

"Is that so?"

"I asked you about us dating, and you still haven't given me an answer. I don't know if you believed me or not, but what I want hasn't changed."

She was quiet. Thoughtful. Interested.

"I'd like to date you. If that's what they call it these days."

She shrugged. "I guess I might as well. I've already spent the night with you."

He hitched his eyebrows appreciatively. "That you have." He squinted at the phone and said, "Joe's on the other line. I have some logistics to work out with him for tomorrow. It's pressing. I'll talk to you later."

She nodded and they ended the call.

What had she just done? Committed to being a girlfriend? Did that make her a cowgirl? She admonished herself for the silliness, but she knew one thing for sure, she couldn't stop her heart from pounding.

***

The gifts kept arriving.

On Tuesday, Addison received a box of bath salts and lotions from an exclusive shop in downtown Forest Hills. On Wednesday, a copy of Stacey Abrams' latest novel arrived. It was personally autographed. She couldn't be more thrilled. On Thursday, the fifth day, she received pillows. Really luxurious ones. She hadn't heard of the brand, so she Googled them and nearly fainted at the price. The attached note read:

Take a nap!

Stone

On Friday, she'd just arrived home from work. She was rushing to change to meet Sienna for dinner when a long truck pulled up. When she opened the door, racks of designer clothes were wheeled into her house. Sienna had been given the heads up, hence their dinner plans. They spent the evening shopping right from the comfort of her couch.

Saturday morning, Addison woke up in a room filled with new clothes. She hadn't had the energy to hang everything up, and then she spent hours on the phone watching a movie with Stone. She picked up her phone and swiped. She had a message from him, advising her a limo would be at her door at noon to pick her up. She could dress as casual or dressy as she wanted to.

Her heart smiled. Another surprise. There was only music, sushi, and rain left. He couldn't make the weather. It was going to be sunny today. She decided not to try to guess. It was too fun being surprised. She went to her kitchen and fixed a cup of fancy coffee and enjoyed a leisurely morning before showering and getting changed.

The limo arrived on time, and she felt like a princess going to the ball. It pulled up to her favorite sushi restaurant. Addison stepped in and the restaurant was empty. That never happened on a Saturday. Candles were lit all around. The tables were moved so that one single table sat in the middle of the floor. Fresh roses in various locations decorated the room. She sat and waited. The door opened and Stone walked in. Addison released the biggest breath she'd ever inhaled. She stood on shaky legs and walked to him. "What are you doing here?"

"Surprising you."

"Who told you I loved this place?"

"Rachel. I've been in cahoots with her and Sienna all week."

He took her hand and kissed it before he pulled her chair back out and had her sit. Stone looked devilishly handsome. He had light skin, but the sun had baked him a solid, toasty brown.

"You got a tan."

"A week in the sun with kids will do that to you."

"How was it?"

"Great. It's always great."

A crew of people came out, rolling a waist-length table with items on it.

Stone took her hand. "Come on. We're going to learn how to make our own sushi."

A chef appeared and they spent the next couple of hours making different kinds of sushi and eating it, or rather she did for the most part. Stone was not a big sushi fan, but he tried a few things. On the way to her house, they stopped for takeout for him—a steak from Fontana's—and went back to her house.

They settled on the couch to watch a movie and eat dessert.

"You know I was impressed with Cole. That Paris proposal was everything."

Stone nodded, rubbing her arm. "Yeah, it was."

"But," she inched closer to him, so they were practically nose-to-nose, "what you did this week was even better. Every day I felt more special than the last. I just…"

Stone raised a hand to stroke the side of her face. "I told you I would handle you with care. That means I *will* make you happy. Do you understand that?"

She nodded. "But tell me. What do I have to do to make you happy?" It was a loaded question. She hoped his answer would be something she could do. Stone's history with women was always in the back of her mind.

"Just be you. That's all this cowboy wants, darlin'."

She folded herself into his arms. If he wanted her, he could have her.

Chapter 19

Stone hated to leave her.

"I'm having a drink with Montgomery. We're talking through a business deal."

Addison nodded. "What kind of business?"

"Nothing for you to worry your pretty little head about."

She put her hands on her hips and cocked her head forward like she was trying to hear clearly. "Did you just say pretty little head?"

"I didn't mean that." He whistled with a long breath. "I need to watch my words."

"Yes, you do."

"The answer to your question is, it's manufacturing. He has a factory in Thailand. I need better pricing on some items I purchase on a regular basis."

"Okay." She folded her arms in front of her.

"I can come back."

"You shouldn't. It'll be late, and you know I have to get up early for church."

Stone noticed the vein in her neck was tight as a drum. He stepped closer. "Are you sure you're okay?"

"I'm fine." She dropped her arms.

He kissed her on the forehead, and she walked him to the door. "I would like to come back."

"I think that would be dangerous," she said, wrapping a curl around her finger. "I've already risked it all with you once. Go to your meeting."

Stone felt uneasiness coming from her. It was in her voice, but he was running late. He'd get to the bottom of it later.

The meeting with Montgomery was a bust. The man had already had too many drinks before he arrived. He also let women interrupt them. Stone wasn't trying to be seen in Forest Hills at a table with a bunch of women, so he ended the meeting and went back to Cole's house. Addison was on his mind. She looked stressed when he left. Maybe she was sad to see him go. He knew he didn't want to leave her. He regretted that he couldn't spend more time in Forest Hills right now. He was heavily involved in the first three weeks of the camp, so he had to be there. He checked his watch. It wasn't too late, so he called her.

"What are you doing?" he asked.

"Lying on my expensive pillow reading my Stacey Abrams book."

He smiled. "How's the story?"

"Very good," she said. "How was your meeting?"

"A waste of time. He was drunk, so we'll meet again," he said, dismissing it. "What time is church?"

"Ten. You want to join me?"

"I already told Rory I'd come to his service. Have you been?"

"No, but I should."

"He could use a few visitors. It's pretty small," he said.

"It's my Sunday in the nursery. I'm committed, but do you want to have brunch after?" she asked.

"I thought you had brunch with your sisters."

"I do, but I can miss one."

"I don't want you to start breaking your family traditions for me."

They were silent for a minute. He wasn't sure if that's what he should have said. Was she supposed to make those kinds of choices for him? Should he expect it? He remembered Cole's words, "Consider each other more than yourself." The Ingram sisters' brunch was a thing they always did, so he figured he was right to not expect her to step away from it for him. "I have an idea."

"You usually do," she teased.

"Come to Mountainville this week. Observe the camp. You need to for the book, and you could get some cow people pics. My staff will pose."

"I have staff meeting on Monday and some training on Tuesday, but I'll see what the rest of the week looks like."

"Diamond Bennett misses you."

"I miss it."

"Addison, I…" he paused.

"What?"

"I had fun today."

"Me too," she replied. "Hey, I'm not getting a dog this week, am I?"

He laughed. "No, and I can't predict the weather either, but I'm working on that."

"I have never felt so special."

"I've never wanted to make someone feel so special."

They talked a few more minutes. Addison yawned and he knew it was time to let her sleep, so he let her go.

Hours later, he was still having trouble sleeping, so he crept down the stairs and went to the museum room. It was a room Lenise decorated for Cole that included all of their deceased father's artifacts from his travels and a collection of photographs. There was one thing he was looking for. His dad's Bible. He found it and took a seat.

He exhaled. "Dad, I wish you were here to meet the love of Cole's life. You would be proud of him."

"He'd be proud of you too," Cole said, stepping into the room.

"I thought you two were out."

"We were. We got in a little while ago." He walked over and looked at the book in Stone's hand. "Dad's Bible, huh?"

"Yeah, I felt like reading. I figured his was…" Stone paused and opened it, "…here."

"I've thumbed through it a few times myself. He took good notes."

"I noticed that." Stone temporarily closed the book. Changing the subject, he said, "Two weeks until the big day."

"Yep."

"You can't wait."

Cole smiled. "I would have eloped in Paris. This is for her."

"She deserves it."

Silence passed between them for a long minute. Cole spoke. "You seem troubled, brother."

"For the first time in years, I wished I lived in Forest Hills."

"The relationship is new. You'll work it out."

"True," Stone agreed. "I guess I didn't realize how easily someone could disrupt my life."

"Don't look at it that way. See her as adding to your life."

"Adding to my stress is more like it."

"I'm sure she feels the exact same way about you. Take one day at a time." He gave him a pat on the shoulder. "I've got to go. Lenise and I are headed out early tomorrow for service."

Stone nodded.

"See what the Holy Spirit has to say," Cole said, pointing at the Bible. Then he left.

His father told him that the book would always open to something he needed to read. As a child, Stone thought that was some kind of Jesus magic. But now as an adult, he realized it simply meant all Scripture was, just as it says in 2 Timothy 3:16, God-breathed and useful for teaching, rebuking, correcting, and training. Stone wondered which of those it was going to do today.

He thumbed the Bible and it happened to open on a page his father had inserted a sticky tab on in Ezekiel. Chapter 36. His eyes went to verse 26 because his name was written next to it in his father's handwriting. He read, "I will give you a new heart and put a new spirit in you; I will remove from you your heart of stone and give you a heart of flesh."

He closed the Bible and then closed his eyes. He repeated in his mind, *I will remove from you your heart of stone and give you a heart of flesh.* He had studied the

Word enough to know that the new heart we received was a result of salvation. But he wasn't sure what God was trying to say to him right now. It would eventually come to him.

The next morning, Stone texted Rory and told him he'd give him a raincheck on service. At 9:50 a.m., he got out of his truck in front of Good Faith Church and stood by the door, waiting for Addison. She, Rachel, Sienna, and Zoe arrived and shortly after, Logan and Harper. He knew Zeke was in North Carolina and Ethan and his daughter went to Rory's church every week.

Addison's radiant smile stopped his heart. He was glad she was glad to see him and that it wasn't a stalkerish idea to surprise her.

After everyone greeted each other, Sienna said, "I guess I'll take nursery duty."

Addison thanked her sister. She took the extended crook of Stone's arm as they fell into step next to each other.

"What about Rory's service?"

"Next time. I couldn't go back to Mountainville without seeing you."

The smile she gave him filled his heart with a special kind of happiness. They found a pew and sat. He'd never attended church with a woman. It felt nice. They shared Addison's Bible, but it wasn't the only thing they shared during the service. They stole glances at each other. Stone held her hand. Having her next to him like this felt like the most natural thing in the world. For a moment, he thought about Nancy. He was fuzzy on the details, but he thought he felt this way about her too. He felt tension rising in his chest and for some reason, the words from his father's Bible came back to him.

I will remove from you your heart of stone.

He glanced at Addison. Did he need a new heart to fully love her? He needed to figure it out because he wasn't going to hurt her. He'd promised he wouldn't.

After service, they all stood talking for a moment. Rachel invited him to brunch.

Before he could respond, Addison interrupted and said, "Actually, Stone and I are going to hang out before he has to drive back. So, I'll see you all later."

He told himself, this wasn't his failed marriage. He could trust Addison. He'd considered her and then she'd considered him. They'd considered the needs of each other. He took her hand and they walked to his truck.

"Where would you like to go?"

"My house. If we go to a restaurant, I'll have to share you with the world. I don't want to do that."

He frowned, but he guessed privacy was better, especially for her. She had a reputation to protect from his reputation.

She squeezed his arm. "Plus, I have it on good authority that in addition to barbecue, you love Mexican food."

He nodded. "I am from Texas. How did you find that out?"

"You asked my sisters about me, and I asked your brother about you. This works both ways."

A smile filled his face and his heart. She was considerate, and that was something he remembered Nancy never was. She was always taking. He chastised himself mentally. *Make this the last comparison.*

"Do you?" Addison's voice broke through his thoughts.

He gave her his attention. "What was that you asked?"

"Do you want Mexican? I have a quick recipe for enchilada pie, and I have all the ingredients."

Stone stroked her face—her beautiful, warm, lightly freckled, honey brown face—and waited for her softness to do what it always did...quicken his heart. *I'm falling in love.* He swallowed and pushed the words aside to answer her. "Let's go whip it up."

In his peripheral vision, he could see her happily snapping her seatbelt into place. He was glad she couldn't see that his hands were trembling when he stuck the keys in the ignition. He was definitely falling in something.

Back at Addison's house, she gathered the ingredients and gave Stone things to chop up and wash while she prepared other parts of the dish. They fell into a comfortable groove working with each other. It wasn't long before the smell of ground beef, tomatoes, garlic, onions, peppers and jalapenos mingled to create an aroma that made his stomach growl. He helped make the salad, which was something he'd never done before. When the dish came out of the oven, the cornbread called to him. He ate more than he'd eaten in a long time. It made him sleepy and lazy. Too lazy to drive, so they cozied up on the couch to watch Zeke's soccer team, the Carolina Sirens, play. The weather had changed, unpredictably so, and a light shower of rain began to fall.

"Look," he said, pointing through the sheers on the window. "It's one of your favorite things."

"And I get to enjoy it with one of my favorite people," she whispered as she nuzzled his ear with her nose. It wasn't long before they fell asleep. Stone woke first. He pulled Addison closer. She placed a hand on his chest and pressed her head under his arm and stretched out alongside of him. He woke her with kisses on her forehead and face. Would all his Sundays be like this if he was in Forest Hills? He hoped so.

"I should go," he said. "I was supposed to leave hours ago."

"I know." She scrunched up her face playfully. "I'm sorry I stole you."

He kissed her hand. "It was nice to be stolen. But I have to roll out."

Addison walked him to the door, and then she remembered she'd packed up leftovers for him, so she dashed back to the fridge and got them.

"See what you can do about getting up my way this week."

"I will," she promised.

He left her house, but his heart didn't. Not at all. Halfway through the drive, he talked himself into calling Zeke.

"Congratulations on the win," he said when Zeke came on the phone.

"Thanks. It was a close one. What's up?"

"Are you happy with the realtor you're using?"

"Yeah, there isn't much inventory in Forest Hills, but we've been looking. We might buy land and build."

Stone nodded. "Text me her number."

"Okaaay," Zeke stretched the word.

Stone appreciated that his cousin didn't ask for more details. But if he had, he would have told him, it was time for him to look at property in Forest Hills. He had no idea what that would mean for his life in Mountainville, but he was going to have to figure it out and soon.

Chapter 20

The first email Addison received for the day was the proof from the article for the bachelors of Atlanta, but with the meetings and conference calls she had back-to-back, it was the last thing she looked at before she left for the day. Putting it off was a mistake.

She popped out of her chair and made breakneck speed to Beth's office. "What is this?" She dropped a printout of the cover on the desk.

Beth picked it up. "'The Bachelor with a Heart of Gold.' I gave it the title, so I remember it."

"Beth, where did you get the information about Stone Bennett's summer camp?"

Beth finished tapping out a message on her phone and put it down. "From you."

"You most certainly did not."

"You put it in the folder. I found it there."

"Since when do you look through my research?"

"You left off a source, so I looked for it. I needed to get this done. You should have told me about it. It's gold."

Addison bit her lip. This was not gold, and it was not good. "I didn't include it in my story. He didn't want anyone to know about the camp."

"Why?"

"Because he doesn't. We can't run it like this. We have to go back to the original cover."

"*We* don't have to do anything. I make the editorial decisions here, and this story will sell magazines."

"You can't do this. It was hard enough to get him in the magazine in the first place. We can't alienate him. I have the Black Cowboy feature coming up."

"He doesn't have to be a part of that story. There are lots of Black cowboys in the southeast."

"Beth, please. I promised him."

Beth cocked her head. "Promised him, before you talked to me about it?"

"This isn't fair. Not to him and not to me. You've taken this story in a completely different direction. If you want to feature Stone Bennett, let's try to do it at a later date…with his permission on the content."

Beth pointed to the printout of the cover. "That is done. Now please review the proof and let me know if you find any typos or punctuation errors."

Addison felt sick. How had she let this happen? "If you run this, take my name off the byline. I didn't write this."

Beth shrugged. Addison knew that meant the byline "staff writer" was fine with her boss. "Close the door on the way out."

Addison was practically hyperventilating when she left the building. Stone was going to be furious with her, and he would be right. She let this happen. Though Beth was stank for changing the story up, she should have never put those files on the server.

She pulled into the driveway of her house and parked next to Sienna's car. She wasn't expecting her sister, and she wasn't in the mood to talk to anyone right now. When she entered the house, she found Sienna in the kitchen, pulling something out of the oven.

"Welcome home," she said, kicking the oven door closed with her foot. "You are about to be the guinea pig for my seafood lasagna."

Addison dropped her purse and reached into the refrigerator for a bottle of Perrier. "I'm not sure I can eat anything right now. Why is this lasagna coming out of my oven and not yours?"

Sienna put the potholders down and planted a hand on her hip. "Somebody had a bad day. Since when do you not want food?"

"You have no idea how lucky you are that you're an entrepreneur. Working for people is...ugh, the worst." Addison kicked her shoes off, pulled her laptop from her work bag and put it on the island before sitting.

Sienna's other hand went to her other hip. "You don't think entrepreneurs work for other people? I plan parties and weddings and events...all I do is work for other people."

Addison dropped her head back. The frustration was overwhelming. She didn't want to have this conversation right now. She didn't want to have any conversation right now. She wanted to be alone. She returned her attention to her slightly annoyed sister and forced herself to be decent. "I didn't mean it like that, but you're your own boss. You don't report to people."

Sienna pursed her lips. "Girl, please."

"Okay, okay. I'm wrong. Give me a break. I was expecting to come home and not have to be social." She raised her hands to her head and rubbed her temples. "But you're here."

"And I have been for many hours. You need to turn around and see your latest gift from Cowboy Bennett."

Addison spun on the stool. There was a large metal and glass structure hanging on the wall in the living room. She hopped off the stool. Before she got to it, a light came on and water started falling inside the glass case. It was a fountain, one that dripped water against stone and marble. She raised a hand to her mouth. It was rain. He'd brought her rain.

She felt Sienna come alongside her. "This is why my lasagna is in your oven. I had to wait for the delivery and installation. It took a few hours."

Addison's eyes filled with tears. "I'm sorry I was so short." She reached for Sienna's hand and squeezed it before letting it go. "Thank you."

"He's been good to you, girl." Sienna said, handing Addison a remote control. She read the controls. They were simple—Power, Fast, Slow, Light. "And coming to church like that. What is really going on?"

Addison's heart sank. What was going on was he was going to be furious.

Sienna continued to question her. "Are you guys serious? I mean like really serious?"

"I think so."

"You're not sure?"

Addison walked back to the island. "I'm never sure." She slid onto the seat. She opened her email and pulled up the proof for the article.

Sienna rounded the corner and removed plates from the cabinet. "What happened at work?"

Addison took a sip of her drink. "My boss added some personal information to the story about Stone. I promised him it wouldn't be included. He's going to be furious."

"What is it?"

"His charity. He wanted to keep it anonymous."

"Doesn't he have the right to contest something said about him?"

"Eh. Yes and no. Not really. Not this. It's true, and it's not bad."

"I suppose there's nothing you can do to change it."

"Beth is being a jerk."

"You've been clear about that for a while."

Addison scratched her head. "It's my mistake. I put the information where she could see it. I just never expected her to rifle through my files. She has never done that before, or at least she'd never changed one of my stories."

Sienna removed a salad from the refrigerator. She fixed two servings and slid one in front of Addison. "Get in front of it."

"I will. I'm going to tell him tomorrow. The article comes out online on Thursday."

Sienna cut into the lasagna and put two pieces on plates. "Cheese and shellfish make everything better."

Addison smiled half-heartedly. She wasn't sure anything could make this better, but she picked up her fork. "Let's see if it will."

Chapter 21

Addison never took sick days. She was never sick, but she'd awakened early this morning feeling like she was having an anxiety attack.

"Coffee," she whispered. "I need coffee."

She pushed herself out of bed and went down the stairs.

As she stood in the living room, holding her favorite mug, drinking the Ethiopian coffee Stone had gifted her while she stared at the rain cascading down the glass fountain, she felt sicker. All he'd done was nice things for her and what had she done? Broken his trust. She had to explain. She finished her coffee, got dressed, packed an overnight bag, and got in her car. She was headed for Mountainville. Telling him in person would be better, and he had invited her to visit to observe the camp. She had an excuse for showing up.

While sitting at a traffic light, she dashed an email to Beth, taking a sick day, and turned her work phone off. Beth hated not to receive a direct call and after their words last night, the woman would be angry, but Addison didn't care. Fixing things with Stone was bigger than this ridiculous story. This ridiculous story she never wanted to do. But then she realized if she hadn't taken the assignment, she wouldn't have gotten to know him better, so it was all a big fat Catch-22.

Her phone pinged a text message. She glanced at it:

Stone: Good morning, beautiful. You must have been tired last night. I thought I'd hear from you.

She smiled and texted him back.

Addison: I was sick. Sorry. Headed to a meeting. What time do you take lunch?

She felt so lame saying she was sorry to not call when he'd given her such an expensive gift. She'd Googled the thing. It cost thousands. Her phone pinged again.

Stone: Noon. Call me.

She dropped the phone and continued the drive. She estimated she'd be there by 11:30. At 11:20, she was pulling through the gate. She'd had security call Swenson, and Swenson was more than happy to let her in.

Once she arrived at the main house, she used the restroom. She was exiting when she heard Stone's voice booming from the kitchen. "What do you need?"

Swenson replied, "You'll know in a minute or two."

"Swen, you call me up here like it was urgent. What's going on?"

Addison crept up behind him and put her hands over his eyes. He removed them and spun around.

"Addy?" He smiled and picked her up off her feet. "Doggone, woman, you got me good."

After he placed her feet back on the floor, she stepped out his embrace. "That was the plan."

"Are you staying for the week?"

She cleared her throat. "I haven't really cleared a week with my boss. We'll see."

"I'll take your bag to your room, Miss Ingram." Swenson left them.

The dimple caught in his cheek when he smiled. "This is the sweetest surprise I've had in a long time."

Addison cried inside. She was going to disappoint him. "It's good to see you too."

Stone took her hand again and kissed it. "I smell like a horse."

She thought, *"But you look like something sweet dipped in caramel."* She said, "Well, soon I will too. You're taking me to hang out with your kids."

"They're going to love you." His excitement was high. "It's lunchtime, so let's eat."

After they ate, Addison spent the afternoon tailing him around the camp. By 3 p.m., the kids climbed in a few wagons and went to the barracks. It was time for swimming lessons and then they'd have dinner. The evening was spent doing wood working projects and leather crafts. They had a full day.

Stone wanted to take her off the property for dinner, but she insisted they stay in. She needed to tell him about the article. She couldn't delay it. They ate on the deck and once Stone put the last of his dessert in his mouth, she said, "I have to tell you something. You're not going to like it."

Stone cocked an eyebrow. He put down his fork and said, "Okay."

"I know you told me not to include the camp in the article, but it's in there."

Stone looked confused at first, but confusion quickly gave way to anger. "What do you mean, it's in there?"

"My editor found my research. She amended my story to include it."

Stone was silent for a long moment. He moved his jaw around like he was trying to pop something back into place. "How did she know about your research?"

"I put the information in a file in the shared drive. I keep all my research there."

He stood. He locked his hands behind his head and walked around the deck for a minute before coming back to where she was. "Are you telling me you were careless?"

Addison stood. "She's never done this to me before. She's never gone through my files. She's never added anything to one of my stories."

"So why me?"

She shrugged. "It's newsworthy."

"Newsworthy." He guffawed. "There's nothing newsworthy in that trash magazine."

Addison swallowed the urge to rebut. She had his anger coming, but she hadn't expected that insult. "There's more."

He cocked his head. "What more?"

"It's the cover feature, Stone. Your picture is on the cover and 'The Cowboy With a Heart of Gold' is the title."

His blood pressure must have hit a high because he turned red. His mother, Diamond Bennett, was said to have descended from Georgia Cherokee natives. She could see that manifest in his coloring right before her eyes.

"I trusted you."

"I'm sorry."

"Sorry isn't good enough, Addison. I specifically told you this was personal for me. If I knew I couldn't trust you, I would never have asked for you."

Addison blinked. She was disappointed in herself, but then she thought about his words. "What do you mean ask for me?"

Stone's phone rang. He reached into his pocket for it and answered. After a few nods and yeses, he ended the call. "I have to go to the barracks. I'll be back."

"Wait. What do you mean asked for me?"

"You're the journalist, Addy. Figure it out." He bolted through the door. She watched him get on a golf cart and drive away like he was in a racecar.

He never would have asked for her. What did that mean? She called Beth.

She received a sour greeting. "Feeling better?"

Addison rolled her eyes. Beth had some nerve. "Not really, but I do have a question."

"Spit it out. I'm having to go over your stuff because I haven't heard from you all day."

"How did I get assigned to interview Stone Bennett?"

"I received a directive from Tom's office. I was told to assign you to his interview because Bennett requested you."

"Why didn't you tell me when I asked you before?"

"Because I didn't see any reason to tell you. Now we've got all this drama so…" Beth paused, and continued, "Does this have something to do with you wanting me to take out the charity bit?"

"No. I just feel a little manipulated by everyone." All this to get her up here so he could get her in bed. That was his original intent and now she wondered, was it still his intent?

Come up.

See the camp.

How manipulative was this man? She had no idea, but she knew her suspicion was not out of the range of possibility. Montgomery spent months sending her gifts and buying her dinners before she eventually slept with him. It was the challenge and the chase for these guys. They liked to win. For all she knew, he and Montgomery were swapping stories about her.

"Addison, did you hear me?"

"I'm sorry, Beth. What was that?"

"I said your families are connected. I guess he knew you two would have the right chemistry."

"Chemistry is right." The disappointment coursing through her veins turned to anger. "He expected to be able to trust me."

"It's public information, for goodness sake. Just because no one publicized it doesn't mean it's a secret."

"He did a good job of keeping it one. The charity is buried in LLCs. No one would have found it unless they were specifically looking for it."

"Well, it's not drug money, and we're not saying anything bad about him. It can't be that big of a deal."

"It is to him, but you know what, we're writers, right? I'll proof it and have it to you in an hour."

"Good. Call me if you have any delays. You know, in case you start projectile vomiting or something."

Addison pulled her laptop from her bag and opened it. Stone wanted her on the story. She was thorough, so he got her.

Chapter 22

One of the kids had hurt himself. By the time Stone reached the barracks, the nurse practitioner he employed during the camp was already wrapping what she said was a sprained ankle. Stone stayed while he waited for his staff to repeat the safety protocols to the kids one more time. He didn't like accidents. They happened, but most were avoidable, so they drilled safety over and over, in case the kids got laxed about doing things the right way.

He didn't go back to the house right away. He went to the stables and took out one of his horses. It was the first time he was avoiding his own house. This was why he didn't let women come. It was his sanctuary. He was determined not to let one of them taint it. Now Addison had brought exactly what he didn't want...an argument. He wasn't going to fight with her. He reached into his pocket for his phone and placed a call that would fix all of this.

After entering the house, Stone went right to his suite and showered. Afterward, he found Addison on the deck.

She turned when the door clicked closed.

"Sorry about that. One of the kids got hurt."

"Swenson told me."

"I'll have to talk to him about telling you everything, especially since I can't trust you."

"Can't trust me?"

"Yeah, I mean, maybe you'll update the story to include a bit about kids being hurt at my camp."

"Stone, don't be ridiculous."

"You're right. It was ridiculous for me to think I could trust a journalist. I hope your promotion is worth it."

She put her hands on her hips and rolled her neck. "I hope it sells like a million magazines, considering what it cost me."

Stone frowned. He didn't expect her to turn the tables on him with attitude. He didn't have to ask her what she meant by that. She was ready to let him know.

"If I had known about what you did, I would have given the story my all."

"What are you talking about?"

She rolled her eyes. "You manipulated me. You called Tom and had me assigned to the interview. For what? So you could get me up here and try to get me in bed?"

"That's not how it was."

"Oh my God. Please. Of course that's how it was."

"I did call Tom, but I wasn't trying to sleep with you."

Addy crossed her arms over her chest. "The last conversation I had with you on the jet was an attempt to get me into bed or wait—it was the restroom on the jet."

"Addison, I was little drunk, and I was flirting. I knew you weren't going to go into the restroom with me."

"But you have been trying to get close to me. For years." She dropped her arms. "We had a whole conversation about my assignment, and you never said, 'Hey Addy, by the way, I orchestrated the entire thing'."

"By the time we had that conversation, it didn't matter."

"What do you mean it didn't matter? Of course it did."

"Okay, so maybe I was trying to just get close to you. What does it matter now? We're at a different level."

She placed her hands on her hips and craned her neck. "Different level? What level? We're in the basement level. You lied to me."

"I did not lie." Stone threw his hands up. "I just didn't tell you everything."

"A lie of omission is still a lie."

"Well, you promised me. You promised you wouldn't add my charity work to the story."

"And I came all the way up here today to apologize for my mistake, but you know what? I no longer feel sorry. I'm a professional. It's an important part of the story."

He didn't know what to say. She was flipping this on him.

"Remember, why you *said* wanted to be with me, Stone. I'm not just another dumb groupie." Addison walked past him mumbling, "I'm going to bed, and I'll be leaving first thing in the morning."

"Addy," Stone called. "We need to talk. Don't go like this."

She kept walking until she was in the house. He followed calling, "Addison, don't go away angry."

But she was angry. When she turned at the top of the stairs to look at him, all he saw was a scowl.

Chapter 23

Addison sat at the desk in front of the laptop. It was done and proofread. It was ready to file with her editor. "Just push send," she whispered. Her finger hovered over the key.

Her phone rang a video chat. It was Rachel. She was holding Christopher on her lap. "And she has my favorite person in the world."

"You aren't home?" Rachel asked.

"No, I'm at Stone's house."

"Really? You saw him Sunday."

"I know." Addison waved at the baby. "Hi, favorite person." Christopher smiled at her. "I thought you were going to Charlotte."

"I was. Zeke had something to do here today, so we're leaving in the morning."

Addison stood and walked over to the bed and sat.

"What is going on up there? You don't look happy."

Addison filled her in on what happened.

Rachel grunted. "What are you going to do?"

"My job."

"Are you sure you don't want to fight Beth one more time?"

"Beth is not going to yield. The cover is hot. It's going to sell more magazines than we've sold in years. Believe me. I know." Addison groaned. "A cowboy with a heart of gold. It's good stuff. I understand why Beth did it."

"Except he likes doing good without recognition. Which, by the way, is honorable."

Addison's heart broke a little. "I know it is. But if he really didn't want anyone to find it out, he shouldn't have agreed to the interview."

"True, but…"

"There's no but, Rachel. I'm doing my job. Stone took the risk of my finding out when he agreed to let me interview him and visit his ranch."

"But honey, the only reason he agreed to the interview was so he could get closer to you."

"I agreed to the feature to get ahead on my job, so it seems we both got what we wanted."

"How do you feel about him?"

"Right now? I feel lied to."

Rachel pulled her shirt up and put the baby on her breast. "I know, but it's not like a *lie*, lie."

"Whose side are you on? Of course it is." Addison paused. "I feel manipulated, and I hate it. You don't know what it's like to give your heart to someone and get cheated on. I feel like I could lose myself with Stone. Now I don't know if I can trust him."

"I know it's scary—"

"It's more than scary."

"I know, but love is about taking risks. You have to be willing to open your heart and let him in."

"He's already in. That's the problem. He's in, and now I find out he's lied to me."

"He manipulated a situation."

"You don't think that's lying?"

"Addison, you were complicit in helping me with Operation Catch Zeke. Do you remember that?"

"That was different."

"How was it different? I wasn't honest with Zeke about why I was willing to marry him. He thought it was so he could get his money, but I wanted to marry him to get him to fall in love with me." Rachel cut her eyes at her. "By the way, that was your idea."

"It was Lauren's idea."

Rachel readjusted Christopher. He wasn't happy with this conversation. "You were right there with her."

"I'm sorry. I don't agree that this is the same. You loved Zeke. You had been in love with him for years. He needed a tug in your direction." Addison raised her hands to her hair and stretched her ponytail. "Stone doesn't love me. He's attracted to me—today. Who knows who he'll be after next week."

"I disagree. I think there's more there."

Addison smirked. "How could you possibly know that?"

"Zeke."

"What?"

"Zeke told me Stone was planning some next level stuff with you. He's all in."

Addison wasn't trying to hear this. "I don't need this stress."

"You guys are just having a fight. Don't give up on him."

"He's a manipulative playboy, and even if I wanted to…he told me he doesn't trust me. What am I supposed to do with that?"

"Give it time. He was angry. He'll get over it. The same way you can get over it."

"What if he doesn't?"

"He will."

Christopher let out an unexpected wail that shocked both women.

"Well, dang, little guy. Let us know how you really feel about this conversation." Addison said, "Go take care of him. I'll deal with Stone."

Rachel nodded. "Pray before you act. This is still new. Both of you are doing the most."

Christopher wailed again and Rachel disappeared from the phone.

She walked back over to her laptop and pulled up the email. She was angry with him, but Rachel was right. She couldn't make what Beth did okay. She couldn't make her own mistake okay. She had to own her mess, so she rewrote the email:

Beth,

I respectfully request that you publish the story as I submitted it. You're correct, Stone Bennett is like family. I don't want to break a promise I made to him. If you choose not to honor my wishes, please remove my byline.

Attached is the completed proof.

Addison

She pressed send.

Seconds later, her phone rang. It was Stone. She stared at it until it stopped ringing. She didn't have anything to say to him right now. She was busy with her emotions which were her own guilt and her disappointment in him. She wanted to be alone. But that wasn't happening. There was a knock on the door, and Stone's voice followed. "Addison, it's me."

She hesitated and then yelled, "Come in."

The door opened. "Not taking my calls?"

She stood. "I was finishing some work."

"Why don't you come down and hang out with me?"

"Aren't we fighting?"

"Not anymore."

"Does that mean you forgive me?"

Stone walked over to her. "No, but I don't want to talk about it anymore tonight."

"I don't want you thinking I can't be trusted."

Stone stood there, legs parted, with his hands on his hips. The muscles in his sculpted arms flexed from tension. He still looked unhappy. He seemed to be avoiding her eyes, but then he raised them. "Don't worry about it. Tomorrow it won't matter."

She was relieved, but wary too. She wanted to switch her feelings about it off, but she was still feeling some kind of way. "It matters to me that you got me assigned to you and didn't tell me."

"It's obvious I'm insane about you now, so what difference does it make that I used an old friend to hook me up with the woman I wanted to get to know better? Heck, isn't that how most people meet people, through friends and relatives?"

"You could have told me."

Stone raised his hands in surrender. "I thought we weren't going to talk about it."

Addison shrugged. "I'm annoyed with you. What else can we do?"

"Let's go down to the barracks," he said.

Addison frowned. "For what at this time of night?"

"Ghost stories. The kids are about to be spooked. It's one of my favorite parts."

She shook her head. "Manipulating the emotions of children…that's your favorite part? So you admit to being an operator."

A laugh broke through his hard exterior. "I know you're not comparing yourself to the kids because lady…" he leaned in and kissed her neck before pulling back. "You are no child."

"We had our first fight," Addison said.

"It won't be the last one. I can be infuriating and so can you."

She walked past him and turned at the door. "Come on. I hate to miss a good story. Let's go."

Chapter 24

The next morning, Addison woke to a series of text messages from Beth. It was early for her. She realized she'd forgotten to ask her if she could hang up here today to get information for the cowboy feature. She read Beth's rant and called her. There was no answer. She popped up, got dressed and went looking for Stone.

He was in the kitchen with Joe.

"I wasn't expecting you this early. Have a sit down."

"What did you do?" She glanced at Joe, realizing she hadn't said hello. She greeted him, and then waited for Stone to answer.

"I'm going to go to the office," Joe said, taking his coffee mug and leaving.

Addison sat. "Last night, you said it didn't matter about the story."

He shoved a piece of toast in his mouth, chewed and swallowed. "Because the same way you got assigned, you got unassigned."

"What do you mean?"

"I asked you nicely to leave my charity work out of the story. You messed up, so I took care of it," Stone said. "Don't worry, your editor gave you credit for your hard work. You'll still get your better stories or whatever you call it in writer-land."

Addison narrowed her eyes. "You buried my story."

"I buried my story." He leaned back against the kitchen island, casual as you please, like they weren't about to fight some more.

"You had no right to do that."

"I thought you didn't write it."

"I didn't."

"So what's the problem?"

Could he actually not see the issue she was having with this? Was he this arrogant?

"Look, Addison, I'm used to having things my way. In this case, I'm thinking ahead. If you'd broken your promise to me, it would affect our relationship. I did us a favor."

"Our relationship? If this is how you roll, maybe we won't have one." She stood.

He grabbed her hand and pulled her back into the chair. "We already do."

Addison growled. "I am furious with you."

Stone raised a hand. "Temper. You know I like a little fire, but next time, just do what I ask you to do."

She stood again. "I can't believe you did this. It's not even negative. It's heartwarming and kind and generous. You could have let it go, but no, you had to go butting into my situation at work. Do you know how upset Beth is with me? She cussed me out in three text messages."

"Forget her."

"She's my boss. I can't just forget her."

He crossed his arms over his chest and shrugged. "Maybe. Maybe not."

She stepped closer to him. "What do you mean?"

"I mean, Tom was disappointed with how she handled things."

"You got her fired."

"She got herself dealt with."

Stone showed no remorse which made Addison's head spin.

He continued, "Beth knew the request for you to interview me came from above her head. She should have considered that when she played with your story."

"Stone…"

"Tom is going to have to pay a lot of money to reset that magazine cover and get it out on time. She made a bad decision."

"I can't believe you would get her in trouble."

He reached for his mug and took a sip like he was talking about getting rid of a pest in the barn. "I didn't get her in trouble. I told Tom to pull me out of the feature. I told him what you told me about what Beth did, so if she's moved or demoted or fired, that's on her. I don't get involved in Tom's personnel business."

"Except you did."

"The mess Beth made by disrespecting you has nothing to do with us, Addy."

For several moments, she stood there, reflecting on the implications of this in the office. It was all bad. People would know. They would blame her. No one there would trust her. "I'm going home."

"Why would you do that?"

"Because I'm not liking you right now."

He put his mug down. "You made a mistake, and I fixed it. Now you're angry with me."

"It was just a story, Stone."

His jaw clenched and she saw the Cherokee blood heat his skin again. "You should have taken better care of what I entrusted to you."

She released a long breath. "You're right. I'm not perfect. Maybe you should find someone who is." She took a few steps away from him, but then came back, pointing to emphasize her anger. "Beth is a pain in the butt, but she's a person like me. She's just another

Black woman trying to make it in an industry that's dominated by men. White men. How dare you do this?"

"If it comes to it, she'll find another job."

"Yeah, because it's just a trash magazine, right?" Addison said. "You know what…this is what I hate about you and…" She paused. "Rich men like you and Tom and…" Montgomery's face entered her mind. She shook her head. "You move us around like chess pieces on a board. You have all the power."

His eyes fixed on her face. She doesn't see lingering anger, only hurt. "You have the power, Addy. I told you that."

"You told me that, but you've shown me something completely different." She sighed. "I need to apologize to Beth, and I need my space away from you."

She went upstairs for her things and came back down. Stone was standing by the door.

"You were supposed to be getting notes for the book."

Addison hated leaving like this, but she should have anticipated she might. After all, the trip up here was about the story. She knew they'd have angry words, but still, she wanted to resolve them without all this. She looked into his eyes. They carried the same regret she knew reflected in hers. Stone was begging her to stay, but she didn't know how to.

What he'd done to Beth was too much. She couldn't just act like it was okay. It wasn't. He was wrong.

"The camp has four more weeks. I'll come back."

"Addison…" Stone stopped her with his tone. "…You can't leave like this."

"I have my car keys this time. Watch me."

She pulled on the knob and walked out the door.

Chapter 25

Addison woke to an insistent ringing phone. She didn't recognize the number, but she answered it anyway.

"Addison, this is Lenise. I know this is crazy rude, but I'm outside your house. I need to talk to you."

Addison looked at the time. It wasn't even seven a.m. "Okay, give me five minutes. I need to get out of bed."

After she washed her face and brushed her teeth, she went down the stairs and opened the door for Lenise. She was wearing a mauve and white polka dot sundress with cute pink and gold sandals.

"Come in. You look way to stressed for a bride who has my sister in charge of her wedding." Addison locked the door and led the way to the kitchen. Pointing at the island, she said, "Have a seat." She went over to her coffee maker. "Can I make you a cup?"

"I'd love one."

She set it to brew two cups, and then joined Lenise by taking a seat. "So, what in the world has you at my house the morning before your wedding?"

"I really need a favor." Lenise paused a beat and then said, "I need you to be my maid of honor."

Addison blinked a few times. She thought before she said, "What?"

"You met my best friend, Stacey, at the shower."

"Yes, your beautiful and very capable friend."

"She's sick. She has chicken pox and they're all over her body—even on her poor face. I didn't even know people still got the chicken pox. I thought everyone took the shot."

Addison was still stuck on the "be my maid of honor" request. She didn't want to be in a wedding.

"They just popped up yesterday. She's contagious and even if she wasn't, she looks horrible. I was devastated about it, but then I thought of you. You helped me and Cole get together. So you've always held a special space in both our hearts."

"I just planned a few dates for you."

"But they were magical."

The coffee maker beeped. Addison hopped off the stool and poured their cups. She placed the cream and sugar in front of Lenise, and let her help herself before fixing her own cup.

"Lenise, surely there's someone else you're closer to."

Lenise blew on her coffee and took a sip. She put the mug down. "Wouldn't do for me to burn my lip before the wedding." She smiled a little. She reached into her handbag and removed a tissue. She patted her eyes underneath. Addison hadn't even noticed how wet they were. She was on the verge of a full meltdown.

"What about other friends and family?"

"I don't have any other friends, and I'm not close to any of my family. We're a small group to begin with...they don't know I'm getting married. I didn't invite anyone."

Addison frowned. "I'm sorry to hear that."

"I want it to be a happy day. I don't want to look out and see a single person who isn't happy for me and Cole. The few people I am somewhat caught up with in my family are haters. They'd just be jealous. I don't want them there."

Addison raised her coffee mug to her lips and took a tentative sip. It wasn't too hot. Lenise followed her lead and drank too.

"This is really good," Lenise said.

Addison looked across the kitchen at the Jamaican Blue Mountain bag Stone had gifted her. It was good. It was the best.

"You're the same size as Stacy, or at least close, so I know the dress would fit without a bunch of fuss," Lenise said. "I wouldn't ask if I weren't desperate to have someone standing up for me. There's nobody else here that makes sense. I want to look back at my pictures and I want them to make sense."

"It's not that I don't want to help you. It's Stone."

"What about him? He's the best man."

"I know."

"You're friends, right?" Lenise's eyes had gone from tearful to hopeful. Addison wanted to kick herself for even bringing up Stone's name. This woman had enough on her mind.

"We are."

Lenise smiled. "Good. I figured it would be okay. I think he likes you." Lenise took another sip of her coffee and then another. She stood. "I know I threw off your morning. I wanted to ask in person. So, I have a long list of things to do. You can stop in this morning at the Banneker's bridal shop, and she'll make any adjustments necessary."

Addison stood and put her mug down.

Lenise pulled her into a hug. "Thank you so much. Sienna will give you the details for the rehearsal and the dinner and everything." She turned and walked toward the exit of the house with Addison behind her.

Once Lenise was gone, she went back to the kitchen and cleaned their cups. She was planning to go to the wedding, but now she had to do the rehearsal and dinner and all of it...with Stone.

Chapter 26

S tone pulled out of the parking lot for the tuxedo shop. Once again, he was glad he was in Forest Hills. Though this time, he needed to see Addison to fix things. She hadn't taken his calls since she left his house earlier in the week. Not even to discuss the book. He needed to explain, but how could he tell her the truth about why he kept his charity so close to the vest without telling her about Nancy? He wasn't ready for that humiliating conversation. Not yet. And if he brought it up, she might just Google and learn the details herself. The story about his dismantled charity was old and mostly buried in other links that were more relevant and newsworthy, but still findable.

His phone rang and he saw it was Montgomery Robb. He lifted an eyebrow and answered it.

"Hey, Stone," Montgomery began, "I'm leaving in a few days. I have to go to Thailand for business. I figured you might be in town for your brother's wedding. Do you have time for lunch?"

"Sure. I was headed to pick up a last minute something for the wedding, but I need to eat before I resume my best man duties."

"Good. I'm walking into Shiloh's. I'll see you when you get here," Montgomery said.

Stone drove the short distance to Shiloh's Grille and joined Montgomery. Once they were settled at a table and in possession of their drinks, they talked about business. The server arrived with their lunches and as he put them on the table, Montgomery said, "I noticed you weren't in the story we did for bachelors of Atlanta. It went live yesterday online."

"I pulled out at the last minute."

"Seemed like you were invested."

"I changed my mind is all. I like my privacy."

"Problem with Addison?"

Stone frowned. "Why would you assume I had a problem with Addy?"

"She can be tenacious when she wants to be." Montgomery picked up his drink and took a long sip. He put the glass down and cocked his head. "Addy. That's friendly."

"We're friendly."

He pitched an eyebrow. "She never let me call her that."

Stone was feeling protective of her. "Maybe she didn't consider you to be a friend."

"I was a bit more than a friend, brother. For a while anyway." Montgomery raised a hand and waved the server over. He barked an order for a refill of his drink.

"What do you mean, more than friends?"

"I mean we dated for almost a year."

Stone fought to keep his composure in front of Montgomery, but he felt like he'd been kicked in the chest by a horse. "When?"

"A couple of years ago."

"I didn't know that."

"We kept it on the low, you know."

Stone felt something rising in him—envy, jealousy, temper. "How did it end?"

"Badly. It was a little more exclusive for her than it was for me, if you know what I mean." Montgomery reached for his drink, finished his first scotch and reached for the beer he'd also ordered. "She's kind of related to you by marriage, I guess."

"Her sisters are married to my cousins."

Montgomery sat up straighter and pulled on his tie. "That makes her family."

Stone picked up his own drink. "No. It doesn't."

"Since you're friendly, maybe you could put in a good word for me. I would definitely try to holler at that again. She was sweet."

Stone frowned. "Don't do that."

"Do what?"

"Call her *that.*"

Montgomery's brows knit together. He shook his head. "I didn't call her *that.*"

Stone stood and tossed his napkin down on his plate. "Yes, you did. You said, 'I'm going to try to holler at *that*'."

Montgomery snatched back his head. "Man, she's my ex, not yours."

"I'm done with this. It was bad idea from the start."

"Look, if you're feeling her, I'll back off. I'm not letting some snatch come between me and money."

Stone's temper rose in his chest so fast, he moved before he thought. He took the edge of the tablecloth and popped it so that everything fell in Montgomery's direction, onto his lap and the floor around him.

Montgomery was wet with soup, water, his liquor and covered in pasta. "What in the...man, what's wrong with you?"

"I would take you outside, but I don't have time to get arrested." Stone reached into his pocket for his money clip. He pulled out a few hundred bills and tossed the money in Montgomery's face. "Here's for lunch. Use the extra to replace that cheap tie."

The server rushed over, mouth hanging open with shock. Stone took more money from his clip and slid it into the man's hand. "I'm sorry about the mess." He turned and walked out of the restaurant.

Chapter 27

Addison couldn't imagine a trip to the emergency room ending in this splendor, but that was how Cole and Lenise met. From the Peter Langner bridal party dresses, to the exotic flowers and special lighting (flown in from Paris), to the vibrant mix of jewel tones, to the whimsical decorations, everything about the wedding was straight out of a fairytale. After being married to an emotionally, physically, and financially abusive man, Lenise Reid had her happily ever after. Second chances—when you got one—were truly a gift from God.

Lenise hadn't lied about not having anyone here for her. The bride's party dressing room was busting with Bennetts—Avery, Alexandria, Victory, and Raven. There wasn't a shortage of good looks in that family. They would fit in with the beautiful décor of the day, but still, it had to be hard for Lenise to not have family attending, or even her best friend.

"I'm so nervous. What if everything isn't perfect?" Lenise stood in the mirror in a stunning, white, custom Jean-Ralph Thurin dress that would be on next month's cover of *Black Bride* magazine.

"It's already perfect. That dress is the show. We'd all need to be naked to get more attention," Addison offered. "Besides, you are marrying Cole Bennett. It was perfect when you woke up this morning."

Lenise smiled. She looked down at the dress for the twentieth time and nodded. "It couldn't be more beautiful. I just wish…"

"Don't do that!" Her friend, Stacy, was set up on an iPad on the vanity in front of Lenise. The poor woman's face was covered in chicken pox. What wretched luck. Wretched for her and wretched for Addison, because the last thing she wanted to do was walk down an aisle today. Her own heart was broken, and she didn't know how to fix it.

She'd been journaling all week. No amount of writing or eating or crying could get her out of this Stone Bennett funk she was in. She didn't even believe she was angry with him anymore. She was angry with herself. She'd sworn off men like him when Montgomery broke her heart. She wanted a simple man, successful of course, but regular.

The sad thing was, even though he was insanely rich, Stone was somewhat simple. The man just liked horses and nature and a good steak. But his reaction to the article was too much. She'd broken his trust, but to ask for the story to be pulled...she didn't understand. Therefore, in her opinion, it was an egotistical desire to control because he could and that—she would not abide with.

Brittney Fairmont, the wedding coordinator, breezed into the room and clapped her hands. "We are ready to proceed." Brittney coordinated Harper's wedding and consulted on Rachel's because she was the guru on getting people down the aisle. She was also the recent victim of gossip because of her very public and painful divorce from her NFL linebacker husband that included a set of outside twins with his jump-off. The scandal was horrible. People talked about it for weeks, but now months later, Addison could still see the sting of pain in the woman's eyes.

That was one of the reasons Addison went to Nicaragua—to hide. She knew people would look at her and know. If she'd given Stone any more of herself, she'd be looking at another condo in Central America right now.

"Addison, dear. You're behind the bridesmaids," Brittney said, waving her over. What thirty-two-year-old called people dear?

Addison put down the water bottle she'd been sipping from and walked across the room.

"You are becoming a serial bridesmaid. When am I going to see you in your own white dress?" Brittney asked. Her tone was sweet. Addison had known her most of her life, so she knew she wasn't trying to be a mean girl, but it was a mean question, or it would be for anyone who was wanting to get married.

"Not everyone dreams of the white dress," Addison replied.

"But you'd be such a splendid bride."

Addison patted her hand and said, "Brittney, we both know, you better than I, that the wedding is one day."

Brittney blinked a few times to clear the disbelief in her eyes. She accepted Addison's bouquet from her assistant and put it in her hands. "You make a lovely maid of honor too."

Brittney showed such grace under pressure. Guilt leaked from Addison's pores. If "hurt people, hurt people" was a person, it was her right now. She didn't have to say that. She needed this day to be over so she could go home and eat ice cream and watch Netflix until Monday morning.

Brittney's assistant ushered them all out into the hall, leaving Lenise alone with Brittney. As soon as Addison entered the hall, she felt him. She stepped closer to where he was standing because he was standing where she needed to be. It was then that she smelled him—crisp and clean and woodsy. He was disgustingly handsome in the tux.

Suddenly, she saw herself in a white dress. The image flashed before her eyes, nearly assaulting her.

Stone's hand was on her arm. "Are you okay?"

Her stomach swirled, lurched actually. She looked into his eyes and parted her lips to speak, but she couldn't say anything. He was staring at her mouth. She remembered his kiss—gentle and warm and practiced and...

"Addison, do you need to sit down?"

She slid her arm out of his grasp. "No. I'm fine." She took a deep breath and released it before saying, "It's a little warm in there." She nodded toward the dressing room.

"Really? We were freezing in ours."

Chocolate eyes burned into hers, hunting up all her insecurities. She was bothered by his presence. Why was he here? "Aren't you supposed to be out there with Cole and Rory?"

Just then, the door opened behind them. Cole and Trinity Bennett appeared under the door frame. Trinity was wearing the same dress Addison had on, but hers had a different design across the top.

"Addy!" She yelled as she swooped between Stone and Addison and gave her a big hug.

When the parted, they just stared at each other. Trinity had gone from a slightly chunky, still tomboyish twenty-nine-year-old to a tall, willowy thin and gorgeous thirty-two-year-old in just the three years since Addison last saw her. She looked elegant—a change perhaps—or maybe it was the dress. It was a wedding. Everything was elegant.

"Trin, I didn't know you were coming."

"No one knew but Sienna. I'm a surprise for Cole and Lenise. There's no way I'd miss my brother's wedding."

"When did you get in?"

Brittney's assistant handed Trinity a bouquet. She raised it to her nose and said, "Last night."

"You could have come to dinner."

She waved her free hand. "That would have spoiled the surprise. Besides you walk down one aisle, you've walked down them all. You know the drill." She put a hand on her hip. "So you're subbing for Lenise's friend. OMGee, what a disaster."

"If I knew you were coming, I would have said no. I'm sick of weddings, or rather being in them."

Trinity stepped back and slipped her arm through Stone's. "So you're working with my big brother?"

Addison and Stone's eyes caught briefly. Addison forced a smile. "As hard as I can."

Trinity glanced between them. She was a quick study. "Oh my God. What's happening here?"

Addison rolled her eyes. She replied before Stone could. "Trin, work is what's going on."

Trinity looked at Stone. She hiked an eyebrow. "Brother, we need to talk after this shindig."

Cole tapped Stone on the shoulder. After he gave Addison one more longing look, he walked off with his brother.

Addison hadn't realized she'd been holding her breath until she let it go.

"I can't believe it," Trinity said.

"Shut up."

"I never would have pegged you for Stone."

"There's nothing going on with me and Stone."

"Girl, lies. Lies. Lies. I know my brother. And I know you, girlfriend."

The overhead music stopped and then the sound of flute music came through the speakers. The procession was beginning.

Brittney physically moved Trinity in front of Addison. "You first."

Trinity nodded, but she twisted her neck in Addison's direction and said, "My future sister-in-law. I love it."

Addison shoved her.

Trinity laughed and everyone stepped forward.

Chapter 28

"I realized men could be good and loving and generous that night. And I know it's easy to say, well he's a practically a billionaire, he should be generous, but money doesn't make you special, Cole Bennett. It's your heart and because of it, I will love you forever. Thank you for making my life whole." Lenise raised a hand and wiped a tear from Cole's face.

Stone's emotions were stuck in his throat. There wasn't a dry eye in the sanctuary, including his. Stone thought his brother's vows were rich, but Lenise's pouring out of her heart made him do one thing—want Addison. She was fighting to look away from him. He was fighting to push the image of her with Montgomery from his mind. Why hadn't she told him about Montgomery?

On his right, his cousin, Jackson, bumped his elbow. It was time for him to produce the ring. He reached into his pocket, smiled, and handed it to Cole. A few more words were exchanged and Cole and Lenise were Mr. and Mrs. Bennett.

After a thunderous applause, the bride and groom walked back up the aisle with the wedding party behind them. Stone had Addison and Trinity at his sides. He realized these were his two favorite women in the world. Trinity had always been the only one, but now there was Addison. Complicated, slightly untrustworthy Addison Ingram. He didn't need this trouble. He'd already fallen for a complicated woman who kept secrets and broke his heart. But here he was. It was too late. She was already under his skin. Deep. She was in his heart—making the blood pump. She was who he wanted—flaws and all.

They stepped into the limo. Before it could pull away from the curb, Trinity said, "I'm getting in the one with the bridesmaids. I need to catch up with people." She stepped out.

Neither of them reminded her there was an order to this thing—that Brittney would flip because she wasn't in this car. They just sat as far as they could possibly sit from each other, both looking out the window. They were behaving like children. Stone decided to put an end to it. He was not childish.

He cleared his throat and pulled on the lapel of his tux. "I've called you four times this week."

"I know." She continued to look out the window.

"You work for me, Addison."

"You're not the boss of me though. You don't own me."

He inched toward her. "When I have something to say about the book—"

She snapped her neck around and sliced him with her eyes. "Was it about the book? Is that why you were calling me?"

He swallowed. His tongue stuck to the roof of his mouth.

"Tell me what you needed to say about the book." She continued to stab him with the intensity of her anger. "I figured that." She turned back to the window.

"You need to stop being angry with me."

"I'm not angry with you."

"No? So you're just sitting here with steam coming out of your ears because your shoes are too tight?"

She groaned and looked at him. "I could kick you."

"I wish you would. At least we'd be doing something other than this."

Addison was silent for a moment. She dug her fingernail into the stem of one of the flowers in her bouquet like she was trying to wound it. She raised her eyes to his again. "You were wrong."

Words were progress. He nodded. "Okay. If you say so. I'm wrong, so I apologize."

She sighed. "If I say so? I guess they don't say sorry where you come from."

He tossed up his hands. "What are you so upset with me about that you would ignore all my phone calls for, Addy? Come on."

"You overreacted. You need to be sorry about calling Tom. For disrespecting my work. For not believing that I just got busy…busy working for you and distracted by…"

Her words trailed off. He was eager to hear them. "Distracted by what?"

"You!" The word flew out of her like a lit rocket. "You and your big life and your big presence and your gifts and text messages." She put the bouquet down and patted the corners of her eyes. "I was distracted by you, and I wasn't paying attention to my work. But Stone, you took it too far."

He hadn't noticed in the low light of the vehicle that her eyes were wet. He felt bad, but she didn't know everything. "I had my reasons."

"Beth was demoted. She wasn't perfect, but she was a good editor, and she earned that position. The people I work with hate me for what happened to her."

"I had my reasons." This time when he said it, he inserted more bass in his voice—intentionally. He wanted the subject shut down. She didn't understand and it wasn't time to tell her everything.

Addison hesitated, seemingly looking for what to say next. "You need to tell me what the reasons are, otherwise, I don't understand. I will *not* understand."

He inhaled deep and let it out. She wanted to fight. He had something he was ticked about too. "Why didn't you tell me you dated Montgomery?"

Addison blinked a few times. "Because it wasn't any of your business."

"Or maybe because you didn't want me to know you actually do like men with a little bit of coin."

She cocked her head like she was about to turn into a raging, Real Housewife of Atlanta on him. "Are you calling me a gold-digger?"

"I don't know. Should I be? He's not even that likeable, so why else would you be with him?"

The limo lurched forward and moved down the street. Addison raised her hands to cover her face for a moment and dropped them back into her lap. "Thank. You." Her voice trembled on each word.

"For what?"

"For giving me a reason to hate you. I needed that." She opened her purse and removed earbuds.

"I don't want you to hate me." Stone reached for her arm. "I want you to talk to me."

She snatched her arm out of his grip. "It's bad enough Lenise has subjected me to social masochism this evening. I won't be handled physically or mentally. Keep your hands to yourself and leave me alone!"

He sighed. "Couples talk through problems." He recalled his brother's words. "They work through the hard stuff. We need to talk to each other, Addison."

"Five minutes ago, I would have said you first, but now that you've accused me of being a gold digger." She wagged a firm finger between them. "I've got nothing to say to you." She stuck the earbuds in and closed her eyes.

Stone sat back and closed his eyes too. He had to reach her, but right now, she was gone.

***

This was the worse night he'd had in a long time. Addison and he had to pose for pictures, sit together, dance together—they were together for hours and yet miles apart. He was glad when it was over. He watched Lenise hug her tight five times in a row. Addison was holding up good for someone whose heart was broken underneath the surface. At least he thought it was. He knew his was.

Cole's hand was on his shoulder. He hadn't heard him come up behind him. "Hey, come with me." They went into the restroom. "What's got you messed up?"

"Nothing. I'm...come on, it's your wedding, man."

"Yeah, it's my wedding, so tell me so I can give you some advice and get back to enjoying my reception. The honeymoon is coming up, bruh."

Stone laughed. He knew his brother and Lenise hadn't been intimate, so Cole was more than ready for this party to end.

"Did you know Addison dated Montgomery Robb?"

Cole fell back against the wall. He raised a hand to his chin and stroked the neatly trimmed hair. "No, but I don't pay attention to that kind of stuff."

"She did. A few years ago."

"And that's an issue because?"

Stone pushed his hands into his pockets. "I think you know why."

"Jealousy?" Cole chuckled. "Come on, man, she's been living her life the same way you have, and we all know you've been living a lot."

"I know that. I just didn't expect...Montgomery. Why didn't she tell me? She knew I was trying to do some business with him." Stone sat on one of the stools in the room. "The guy is a jerk."

"I'm sure he showed her a different side of himself. Some people can do that. At least she got away from him."

"She should have told me."

"Maybe. Maybe not. Where are you and Addison with this relationship of yours? What happened after you guys hooked up? Are you a couple, or have you made a friends-with-benefits arrangement?"

"What do you mean by hooked up?"

"The night you stayed at her place."

Stone raised a hand to play with a cufflink. "It wasn't what you think."

"No?"

"We talked…for hours and then we fell asleep."

Cole jerked his head back. "Oh."

"I could have made something happen, but she got emotional you know—like she was afraid of me. I don't know how to describe it. We were kissing and then something in her eyes told me that making love to her would be wrong, so I backed off."

"So you've seen how she responded to you, but you're in here being upset about one of her exes? He probably messed her up. Some men can really do a number on women. Trust me, I went through it with Lenise."

Stone sighed and stood. "Women can do the same to us."

"I can't deny that." Cole walked to the mirror. He raised a hand to smooth his eyebrows and adjust his bowtie. "But we're talking about her right now. If she's scared, the best way to help her through it is to assure her that you are who you say you are."

Stone joined him at the mirror. "She's not even talking to me right now."

Cole pointed an index finger at Stone's chest. "You can still tell her. I told Lenise."

Stone's frown deepened. "Without some kind of situation that prompted it?"

"Yeah. I told the woman how I felt. If she's angry, this might be the best time. The words, 'I love you' go a long way. You get mad mileage from them."

Stone's eyes rolled up. "I didn't say I was in love."

"You didn't have to. It's obvious." Cole patted him on the shoulder. "Come on out here and toast me again so I can get on to my honeymoon."

**

An hour later, Stone sat behind the wheel of his car.

Montgomery Robb.

He could only imagine what a jerk like him had done for Addison's confidence. No wonder she was so guarded. He thought back to the story she wrote before she left for Nicaragua. She was dealing with heartbreak. That was obvious. Was it because of Montgomery or someone else? The thought of anyone hurting her set his blood to boiling.

So why are you hurting her?

He groaned against the voice in his head. "I'm not," he replied. He didn't know if he was talking to the Holy Spirit or his conscience. Sometimes they felt like the same thing, but he hadn't hurt Addison in the way Montgomery probably had. She was angry about the article fallout, but that was just her ego, not her heart. Not really.

He called her phone. To his surprise, she answered, but she didn't speak. He guessed she still wanted him to go first. "Are you home?" he asked.

"Don't bother to come here. I'm not letting you in."

"I need to apologize for real. Please, Addison."

"You called me a whore."

He closed his eyes. This wasn't going to be easy. "No, I didn't."

"What do you think a gold-digger is?"

"I'm outside. Let me in."

She ended the call. Stone walked to the door. It took a long time for her to open it. He wasn't sure she would, but he finally heard the deadbolt turn before it swung open.

"The only reason I'm letting you in is to tell you that I'm not going to write the book. You need to find someone else."

He nodded. "Okay."

"I'll get you a check once I deduct the amount you owe me for the research. I'll send all the digital files to you."

He stepped into the house and made his way through the foyer and into the living room like he owned it.

"You're going the wrong way," she called behind him.

Stone heard the door close and then seconds later, she was standing in the living room with him. "You're right." He stuck his hands in his pockets. "I've been going the wrong way for a while."

Addison folded her arms over her chest. The fountain he'd gotten her was running. It added a peaceful serenity to the room. It was the perfect backdrop for the conversation.

"I'm sorry I overreacted about the article."

She dropped her arms. "Was that so hard?"

"Yeah," Stone said. "Because I don't ever have to apologize to anyone." He sighed. "Horses don't talk back, Addy. I've been talking to horses for a long time." He stepped further into the room, removed his jacket, and sat down.

Addison walked to the chair across from him and sat too. "I don't like controlling men. I don't like what you did."

"I keep telling you I had my reasons and now it's time for me to tell you what the reason is." He took a deep breath and dove into the story about Nancy and the baby.

Addison's mouth had been open, she closed it now. In her eyes, he saw empathy, not pity. "I'm sorry. What she did was horrible."

"Believe me…the lie about the baby…it felt like a bull charged me right in my gut." He loosened his bowtie and fell back against the cushion.

"I'm so sorry that there are women who do things like that."

Stone sighed again, this time heavier. "That's not all of it." He hesitated. "We set up a charity together.

Cowkids. It was similar to the program I have at the ranch, but it was in the inner city. The kids were going to learn to ride horses and swim. There was even going to be a community garden. We…" he paused. "…maybe I, wanted them to learn how to grow their own food. They lived in a food desert."

"We were going to have an annual rodeo. Everything was set to begin. My ex, Nancy, had written grants and gotten money from all kinds of organizations in the community and the state. The mayor was on board. The kids were signed up and then…" He paused for a heavy exhale. "She stole all the money. Every dime. I was the face of the whole thing, so I was the one who had to answer for it—publicly anyway."

He paused again. "It was bad, Addison. I had to get lawyers and pay back the money. That wasn't the hard part. I was able to borrow from my inheritance, but the publicity. My name was dragged through the media all across the northeast."

He realized he was wringing his hands, so he dropped them on his thighs. "I finally got the nerve up a few years ago to do this thing I always wanted to do. I didn't want it ruined or sullied. I didn't want anyone to find out I'd done this before and failed. I didn't want people calling me a thief, or even knowing I was just plain dumb. I was afraid your article would open that can of worms back up."

Addison's eyes brimmed with tears. "I'm so sorry."

"It's not your fault. It's not." He shook his head. "Anyway, that's why I started bull riding in the rodeo. I think I wanted to get hurt. I wanted something to hurt more." He stood and walked to the fountain and stared at it. "I swore I would never fall in love again. I let my heart turn into stone."

He turned from the fountain and walked to her. He got on his knees and took her hands. "I'm a proud man, Addison. I hate being made a fool of."

She interlaced their fingers together. They sat there for a while, looking at each other. He could tell she had something to say, but he didn't want to push her for her thoughts.

Finally, she cleared her throat. "If it helps you to feel better about being dumb, I've been made a fool of too. Not publicly, but Montgomery played me."

Stone felt his temper rising again. "Tell me what he did so I can beat him up properly."

"I don't want you to beat him up."

"I almost did yesterday. I restrained myself. I didn't want to go to jail with the wedding and all."

She looked away from him and then turned her eyes back to his. "So that's how you found out."

"We had lunch."

She tilted her head with interest. "What did he say?"

"Just that you guys dated a few years ago."

"He was cheating on me. Probably the whole time. I caught him. I was devastated."

"Is that why you went to Nicaragua?"

She nodded.

"I said what I said about you and Montgomery because I'm jealous. I'm jealous that any man has touched you. I know that's insane. It's wrong and sexist." He admitted. "I saw fire when he told me that, and then he had the nerve to say he wanted you back."

She rolled her neck. "As if he could ever stand a chance."

"Are you sure he couldn't?" Stone chest hurt just asking the question. "You get all tense when you're around him. Are you sure you're not still in love with him?"

She laughed. "God no. He's long out of my system. I think it's just that he reminds me of a failure." She bit her lip before speaking again. "I could ask you the same question. Do you still love your ex?"

Stone shook his head. "God no. She's long, long been out of my system. She definitely reminds me of a failure." He laughed and she laughed with him. "There's only you in here, Addison." He pointed to his chest. "I'm in love with you." He stood and pulled her to her feet.

"Love me? Are you sure?"

She seemed shocked and he had no idea how she could be. Couldn't she see? Couldn't she feel his heart yearning for her? "I'm sure." Their eyes met and held before he continued, "You don't have to feel the same way. You don't have to say anything you're not feeling, or are not ready to say."

She shook her head. "It's—"

He put a finger over her lips. "This conversation is about me being honest with you. I knocked on your door tonight." He pointed toward the entrance. He paused for a moment before saying, "I have spent my life grieving one thing or another. My mother's death. My father's death. Nancy's betrayal. And because of that, I've stayed emotionally disconnected. But I'm tired." His eyes filled with tears. "I've reached the threshold on walking away. I have to stay in this."

"You sound like you're in pain." Addison raised a hand and swiped the tear streaming down his face.

"I am, because I don't know if you want me the way I want you. I told you before. You have all the power."

Addison stroked his cheek. He took her hand, turned his head so his lips touched her skin. He kissed her palm. "All of it."

Epilogue

One month later...

Addison sat up in the bed and looked across the room that was no longer a guest bedroom, but her official visitor's suite at Diamond Bennett Ranch. She stood, stretched, and pushed the remote to open the blinds. Then she went into the bathroom, brushed her teeth, and washed her face. She also pulled off her bonnet and untwisted her hair. Stone was probably out of bed already. He was likely down on the ranch somewhere, but she was going to video call him and get him back up to the house now. She had something to say, and it couldn't wait.

Before she could place the call, there was a knock at the door. She walked to it and pulled it open. She was shocked to find Stone standing there with a tray in his hands. She stepped aside and let him in.

"What are you doing up already?" he asked. Before she could respond, he cocked his head toward the bed. "Back in you go. I have a whole thing planned."

Amused by his effort, Addison giggled, jumped back onto the bed, and pulled the comforter up to her neck. "Do I need to pretend to be asleep?"

He followed her. "That would be helpful."

She pressed her head into the pillow. Closing her eyes, she waited.

She felt Stone's approach before he whispered, "Sweetheart, wake up."

Addison's eyes popped open. She faked a yawn and sat up. "Oh, Stone," she played along, looking at the tray like it was the first time she'd seen it, "you shouldn't have."

"It's Saturday morning. You've worked hard all week. You deserve breakfast in bed." He slid the tray forward and Addison picked up the fork.

The food did not look like any food she'd ever had in this house. Which meant it didn't look good. The toast was slightly burned. The bacon was raw, and the eggs were runny and greasy looking.

She picked up the toast and forced a bite.

"Try the coffee," Stone said, handing her the mug. "I think I got that right."

She half smiled and accepted it. "I can only hope."

Stone took the tray away and set it on the desk. Addison took a sip of the coffee and put the mug on the end table. He had gotten that right.

"I didn't say I could cook. I said, 'I'd know I was in love if I *wanted* to cook for a woman on a Saturday morning'." He leaned forward and pressed his lips to hers. "I've been waiting for you to get up here on a Saturday."

He climbed into the bed, and she wrapped her arm through one of his. He removed a stack of index cards from his pocket. "I know you're used to doing the interviewing, but I have some questions for you."

Addison pulled her arm out of his and propped herself up on her elbow. "Okay. Fire away."

Stone read the first card. "What is your biggest turn-on?"

Addison snatched her head back. "So you just diving right in on a sister."

"You know I like it straight, no chaser."

Addison twisted her lips for a moment as she thought but it wasn't for long. "A man who isn't afraid to get his hands dirty, but, at the same time, knows how to dress up for a night out on the town."

"Doggone if that don't sound like me." Stone leaned forward and kissed her again. Then he cleared his throat before reading another card. "You know you're in love when...?"

She pursed her lips again before speaking. "When I want to see him first thing on Saturday morning, even if he trashed the breakfast."

He laughed. "That's a good answer."

"Yes, it was," Addison said, feeling pleased with herself. "Next."

"What, ma'am, is the key to your heart?"

She hesitated again, merely for dramatic effect. She didn't have to think about the answer at all. "Kindness. Honesty. Generosity. Humility. I want a man who prays and reads the Bible every day because he has a personal relationship with Jesus. He'll need that to deal with me."

Stone nodded. "Okay, and when you meet a man that has all those qualities and habits, what are you going to do?"

"That's easy," she said, sitting up on her knees. "I'm going to love him right back. The way I love you, Stone Bennett."

Stone cocked an eyebrow and took her hand. He kissed it. "Is that so?"

"That's been so. That was so before you told me how you felt about me."

His brows knit together. "What took you so long to say it?"

"I was using my power for..."

He snatched her to him. "Torture!" He tickled her and she rolled away from him, but he pulled her back. "Are you sure?"

"I have never been surer of anything in my life."

Stone smiled. "Good. I'll be right back."

He hopped off the bed and left the room. Minutes later, he returned with a basket holding the most beautiful, black Pomeranian puppy she'd ever seen. The dog had a big, red bow around his neck. It was practically bigger than he was. Stone walked to the bed and put him in her lap.

Addison fell in love with him instantly. "I can't believe you did this…" she looked at the puppy, pet him and said, "Hi, you. Omgosh, I'm so glad to have you. What's his name?"

Stone shrugged. "*She* is yours. I didn't name her."

Addison looked into the puppy's eyes. "How about we call you Maya? I'll name you after my literary shero."

"There's one more thing."

She continued to rub Maya's fur. "More?"

Stone reached for the dog's bow and removed it from her neck. There was a long, red string attached to it with something on the end. The sunlight streaming through the window hit it at an angle. That's when she realized it was a ring. Her breath caught in her throat. It was the largest solitaire, cushion-cut diamond she'd ever seen. All she could do was stare. She couldn't believe her eyes.

"I've been waiting for you to tell me you love me." Stone untied the ring. He got on his knees. "Addison Ingram, I don't want to be a bachelor anymore. Will you be my wife and my forever person?" He slid the ring onto her finger.

Addison stared at it for a few moments before looking into his waiting eyes, those beautiful, chocolate eyes she'd come to love so much. Her emotions were all over the place but in her heart, she was sure of her answer. She flung her arms around his neck. "I will." She released him and looked at her ring again before putting her hands on the sides of his face. "I will be your forever person." Their lips met for a passionate kiss.

All They Wanted

Book 5 – Bennett Family Series
Ethan Bennett and Lauren Ingram's story.
Coming September 21, 2021

Lauren couldn't stop pacing.

Her nerves were worse than shot. They were shredded. Completely. She moved back and forth. Forth and back. She moved like she was doing so to music until a car engine sounded outside. She dashed to the window and looked out.

Harper.

Finally.

She pulled the door open before her sister had a chance to ring the bell.

"Why aren't you dressed?" Harper asked, stepping in. "The party starts in an hour. There's traffic."

She knew she needed to be dressed. She'd asked Harper to pick her up, but she was paralyzed. She couldn't get out of her bathrobe.

Harper looked around. "What is this place?"

"It's my condo," Lauren replied. "I'm renting it."

Harper frowned. "Why aren't you staying at the house, or with me, or Rachel or—"

"Because…" Lauren's lip trembled, "…I've been here for a few weeks."

Lauren watched her sister's mouth drop open. Harper stuttered through her question. "Weeks? Why?"

"I've been in Georgia since February."

Further stunned, Harper blinked a few times like she was counting back the months from September to February and registering the implications of what Lauren was saying. "Since before my wedding?"

"Yes."

"But you didn't come."

"I couldn't."

Hurt filled Harper's eyes. "Why?"

"Because I've been lying, Harper. I've been lying to everyone." Tears fell down Lauren's cheeks.

Harper walked to her and wrapped her arms around her. Lauren sobbed.

"Honey, what's wrong?"

She pulled herself out of Harper's arms. "He's going to hate me for what I've done."

"Who? Who's going to hate you?"

Lauren raised a hand to wipe her eyes. "Ethan. He's going to hate me forever, and he should."

Other stories in the Bennett Family series.

All She Wants – Cole and Lenise – Book 1

All He Needs – Zeke and Rachel – Book 2

All They Need – Logan and Harper – Book 3

If you've read everything in the Bennett Series, please consider my bestselling Restoration Series (Book 1 – The Winter Reunion) or my Second Chances Series (Book 1 – Breaking All The Rules) or The Jordan Family (Book 1 – Give A Little Love).

If you enjoy woman's fiction with romantic elements, consider reading my *Black Expressions* bestseller An Inconvenient Friend and the four books that follow in the series (What Kind of Fool, Righteous Ways, Almost There, and Shame On You.)

Also, consider joining my newsletter for upcoming book announcements and my website www.RhondaMcKnight.com

.

Give A Little Love

Chapter One

"Jesus is the reason for the season." The D.J. from Love 101 FM's smooth voice crooned from the stereo speakers on the table next to her. Brooke Jordan flipped the power button to off before he could say another word. Even though Jesus was the reason for the season, her Christmas was going to be *stank* with a capital S. There was no getting around that fact.

Brooke pushed the plantation shutters on the windows open to let in the sounds of the reggae influenced Christmas music rising up from below. She couldn't believe she was spending Christmas week in Montego Bay, Jamaica. It would have been perfect if she wanted to be here, but she didn't. She wasn't on vacation. This wasn't a pleasure trip. Brooke had drawn the short straw in a staff meeting, so she was stuck working. *Stank*, she thought, *stank on steroids.*

She leaned against the windowsill, closed her eyes and inhaled a long, intoxicating breath of ocean air. Every aspect of the island was paradise: the weather, the ocean views and the food. There was no doubt about it. But no place was paradise when you wanted to be somewhere else. Brooke opened her eyes and squinted to see a couple further down the beach. They lay in the sand, making out or maybe even making love. Honeymooners, she knew. She'd seen them arrive a few days ago. Brooke watched as they arrived and others left. She remembered how it was for her when she had honeymooned on an island. She'd been in love like that. She had made love on the beach and then less than two years later, she was signing divorce papers. She tried not to hold it against the entire Caribbean, but there were too many reminders of her loss. She wanted to go home. Today!

Brooke's cell phone vibrated in her pocket and then she heard a chirp. She recognized the familiar beeping ringtone she'd assigned to her parents. She answered. "Hello. You're early." Brooke noted it was seven a.m., which meant it was six o'clock in Charlotte.

"I wanted to get you before you left for work."

Resting an arm on the windowsill, she said, "You made me nervous for a moment. I thought there might have been some kind of emergency."

"There is an emergency," Evelyn Jordan replied. "My daughter isn't going to be home for Christmas Eve dinner."

Brooke sighed. No one was more disappointed than she that on the only holiday her family emphatically made sure not to miss being together, she was four hours by plane away. There was just no way to get to Charlotte, have dinner with the family, and get back to the island on the same day. She had to work on Christmas Day.

"I'll be home for New Year's Eve," Brooke offered, knowing it was no consolation prize for the annual dinner with her grandmother, parents, six siblings, in-laws and nieces and nephews. She would be the only one missing this year. Her brother, Gage, had returned from a tour in Afghanistan and would be with the family for the first time in two years. Her heart ached and she knew it wasn't just about the family dinner. She'd been away from her family and friends for far too long. With the ridiculous number of hours she had to put in on the project, she hadn't had much time to even socialize and meet other people. Not that she probably would have taken the time to do that either. Brooke was on the verge of sliding into a state of depression and she knew it.

"Is the company sponsoring a dinner for the staff?"

Brooke moved through the large living room of the corporate apartment and entered the kitchen to start the coffeemaker.

"No. Everyone is gone. I mean the people who are still here live on the island. The ex-pats are home. There are two analysts and me. We don't need more. We babysit the system."

"Well, maybe you can make dinner. You could invite the analysts. Is one of them nice looking?"

Brooke shook her head. Not more matchmaking. "Mother." Using "mother" was a sign that she was getting annoyed.

"I'm sorry. I was wondering if a change in environment might…" her mother stopped herself. "Never mind that. You could invite them anyway. People get lonely during the holidays."

Brooke didn't respond. People get lonely at Christmas. Forget people. She was lonely. Last year, she was married. Now, she was divorced. Last year, she was with her family. This year, she would be alone. Last year, she was pregnant. This year, she had no child. She didn't care about what other people needed. She had needs of her own.

"Sweetheart, don't they kind of work for you?" her mother's voice broke through her thoughts.

"Not technically. I'm the team leader. It's not the same as being the boss." Brooke fought to keep a sigh inside. She had explained the nature of her work to her mother several times, but for some reason the details weren't processing. "Anyway, we can't eat together. First off, one has a girlfriend he's spending time with and the other guy is, I don't know, anti-social. I hardly know him. Secondly, if I'm home, they're managing the system. We have to be there for the eighteen hours of the day that we're up."

"It seems such a waste not to be able to entertain. You have that big place and the kitchen is lovely."

Brooke did a visual sweep of the space. Her mother was right. She was in a two-bedroom apartment that slept six adults comfortably. The kitchen was fully equipped with every modern convenience a person could use. The community had three swimming pools, a hot tub, sauna, a fitness center, and it had the added bonus of being directly on the beach with gulf views from nearly every window she'd seen. The company had spared no expense and Brooke was glad. The hotel she had lived in for the first few weeks had gotten old fast.

"I'm not interested in cooking for myself. Freeze a plate for me. I'll eat it when I get home. There are more than enough restaurants for me to stop in at. You know I love the local food."

Her mother conceded. "Okay, sweetie, I know you have to get to the office, so I'll let you go. What time will you be home this evening?"

"Same as always. Around eight."

"You've been working too hard."

"I make good money and I like my job. I can Skype with you guys during dinner. It'll be like I'm there."

Brooke heard the smile in her mother's voice. "It will. I'll take that. Your grandmother reminded me that I need not complain. I have living children. That's a blessing."

She smiled at her grandmother's wisdom and the not-so-subtle message behind it. "Stop complaining when you're blessed." That's what she always said when Brooke moaned about something.

The coffee maker beeped, and she received a text message from her driver that he was outside. "Gotta go. Love you, Mama and tell Daddy I love him too."

"Oh, Brooke, there's one more thing."

She knew it. Her mother never called this early in the morning unless something was up. "Sam called."

Brooke rolled her eyes.

"I didn't want to bring it up. It's not the first time." Her mother paused. "I thought you should know."

Brooke swallowed her contempt and tried to keep her voice even. "Thanks, Mama. I received an email. I'll go ahead and see what it says."

"That's probably a good idea," her mother said. "Have a good day, baby."

Brooke forced a smile into her voice. "I will."

They ended the call. She'd lied to her mother. Brooke had already deleted the email without opening it, and she'd deleted the others that came before that one. She pushed thoughts of Sam Riley from her mind the same way she pushed the delete button. She was not going to let rancid memories ruin her day.

She poured her coffee, popped the lid on her travel mug, grabbed her bags and left the apartment.

"Good mornin', Ms. Brooke." Desmond, the company's full-time driver, opened the door to the company van and helped her into the back row.

"You're cheery this morning," Brooke replied, getting settled into her seat.

He closed the door and went around to the front and climbed inside. "It's almost Christmas," Desmond shrieked happily. "Can you believe it'll be here in less than two days?"

Brooke took a long sip of her coffee and bit her lip after she felt the sting of the burn. It was still too hot. "I've never been away from home for Christmas, so it doesn't really feel like it to me."

Desmond shrugged like her woes meant nothing. "Christmas is wherever you are. You get a tree and play some Christmas music and make a little holiday for yourself."

Brooke chuckled. "A tree?"

"They have plenty in the market. If you want, I can pick one out and set it up for you when you come home this evening. It's no trouble."

Brooke smiled. Desmond very respectful and professional, but he had been trying to get in her apartment for some reason or another ever since she arrived on the island.

"There's a nice tree in the lobby and another out on the beach. We have one at work that I can enjoy too. It's not a big deal." She pressed her coffee cup against her lips and her lie and looked out the window for the remainder of the drive from her apartment to the office building. The trip was less than three miles, but it took thirty minutes because Montego Bay's traffic was gridlocked. Just like it was at home in Charlotte. Where there was work, there was congestion. She surmised you couldn't escape it.

They turned off Sunset Boulevard onto Southern Cross Boulevard. Desmond pulled in front of the tall, 55,000 square foot complex that was the home for Global Computer Systems. GCS provides business process outsourcing and information technology solutions for commercial and government clients. Brooke's position as business analyst was to maintain the servers that processed electronic benefit card transactions for a government nutrition program. The client's customers had access to the benefits on their cards 24 hours a day, so the system had to be online 24-7 or it was a customer service nightmare. They'd had those nightmares in the past. In order to ensure that the company didn't lose the government contract, GCS went through a massive technological upgrade in all the offices where they outsourced, which included this location.

Desmond opened the door on her side. Brooke stepped out and reached in for her bags.

"Would you like me to come get you for lunch?"

"No, thanks. I'll get something up the street," she replied, referring to the multitude of area restaurants she had to choose from.

"You text me if you change your mind about that tree."

She smiled. "Not likely. Even if I were inclined, I don't have time."

"You do keep long hours, but at least you have some more help today."

Brooke wasn't sure what he meant by that. She tilted her head forward. "More help?"

"I picked a gentleman up at the airport last night."

Brooke wasn't aware of anyone else joining them. She wondered who had been given the daunting task of showing up the day before Christmas Eve. She knew she was being replaced in a few days so she could go home for a week, possibly for good. But she'd assumed the coworker that was replacing her wouldn't arrive until after Christmas. She also knew it was a woman, not a man.

She was way too curious to wait to find out who the mystery person was. She took a few steps toward Desmond and asked, "Do you remember his name?"

"I don't. I was told to meet him and hold up the company card," Desmond said. "It was late, and he had to take a connection in from Kingston, so he was tired. He fell asleep in the car on the way from the airport."

Brooke nodded. If he'd flown to Kingston, he hadn't come from the Charlotte office.

Desmond continued. "He was here before, I think. But he either walked to work or rented a car. I didn't drive him."

Brooke shrugged. "I guess I'll find out today."

"In a few minutes," Desmond added. "He asked for an even earlier call than you, so he's already here."

Brooke nodded again. "Thanks for the heads up. I'll see you later."

Desmond smiled. As was his habit, he climbed in and waited for her to clear the entrance of the building. As she was coming in, Brooke caught sight of a woman that she'd seen many times in the square near the restaurants and shopping areas. She appeared to be homeless on most days, choosing to sit on the ground or lie on the waist high concrete walls that enclosed the main walking areas. Two of the security guards had her, one under each arm and were escorting her out of the building.

One of them tipped his hat and the other greeted her, "Good morning, Ms. Jordan. I already turned the key in the elevator, so you can go right up."

"What's going on?" Brooke felt sorry for the woman. She looked like they were manhandling her a bit.

"She knows there's no trespassing," the other guard replied.

"Wait." Brooke stopped in front of them. She reached into her handbag and took out some Jamaican dollars she'd had converted from U.S. currency. It was more than enough to feed the woman for several days.

"Ma'am, no need," the guard stated.

"I know you're doing your job, but please turn her loose," Brooke insisted. They did as they were instructed. Brooke took the woman's hand and pressed the money into it. "Get something to eat okay."

The woman looked down at the bills and cackled. "I thank you, Ms. Brooke, but I'm not hungry."

Brooke was taken back. Her first name. "How do you know---?"

"I heard the people you work with call you that," she said. "You've got a good heart. God is going to bless you with love."

Brooke opened her mouth to speak, but then closed it when she realized she didn't really have anything to say. Brooke was a bit uncomfortable with the lady's words, especially since she was a stranger that appeared to need someone to speak into her own disheveled life. But she wasn't going to assume that God wasn't using her. What was that scripture her grandmother quoted about "entertaining angels unaware"? So even though she'd simply wanted to make sure the woman ate and wasn't thrown out like trash by the security guards, Brooke paused to consider the stranger's words.

"Any idea where I'm going to find this love?" Brooke fought to hide the hint of sarcasm that threatened to coat her tone.

"You've already found it," the woman replied. "Just give a little and life will give back."

Brooke had no idea what she could be talking about. Other than giving out of her wallet as she just had, there wasn't any other opportunity for her to share with anyone. Brooke nodded her understanding and watched the woman push through the revolving door and exit onto the street.

One of the guards escorted her to the waiting elevator and continued to hold the doors open while she stepped in.

"She's a crazy lady. Been cuckoo since I was a kid. Keep your money the next time."

Brooke supposed the guards were right. They would certainly know better than she. But her grandmother had taught her that if we have the time of day for a dog, we have it for each other. Besides, the money was nothing. She made plenty.

The elevator doors closed. She pushed the button for the fourth floor of the building where the offices for I.T. were housed. The main server was on the basement level. The three intervening floors comprised a call center. Those spaces were empty today because it was Sunday. Very few call center staff worked on Sunday and those that did were in the United States offices.

Brooke heard her cell phone beep. She reached into her purse to remove it and felt a sharp bump against the bottom of the elevator car right before it paused. The elevator seemed to reboot and start again. She made a mental note to tell security to contact building maintenance and a second note to remind herself to use the other elevator until they fixed the problem. She looked down at her phone, opened the text message and read the words:

Aren't you usually at your desk by now?

Her heart started racing. She cleared the screen and dropped the phone back into her purse. The elevator doors opened. The late-night arrival Desmond had spoken of…

"Good morning, Brooke. I've missed you."

Brooke let out a long breath. Christmas just got upgraded to ratchet.

About the Author

Even as she earned degrees in Textile Technology, Organizational Leadership and finally a master's degree in Adult Education, **Rhonda McKnight's** love for books and desire to write stories was always in the back of her mind and in the forefront of her heart. Rhonda loves reading and writing stories that touch the heart of women through complex plots and interesting characters in crisis with Christian and inspirational themes. In 2015, she was the recipient of an Emma Award for best Inspirational Romance from the Romance Slam Jam literary organization. She is also a member of the board for *The Christian Book Lover's Retreat.*

www.ChristianBookLoversRetreat.com and *Black Ink Charleston* **www.BlackInkCharleston.org/**

Rhonda writes from the comfort of her South Carolina home with hot tea, potato chips and chocolate on hand. At her feet sits a snappy, little dog. She can be reached at her website at www.RhondaMcKnight.com and on social media at the following locations:

www.facebook.com/BooksbyRhonda
www.facebook.com/groups/RhondaMcKnight
www.instagram.com/AuthorRhondaMcKnight
www.twitter.com/RhondaMcknight